Seducing MRS. ROBINSON

BY
RACHEL VAN DYKEN

Seducing Mrs. Robinson
A Bro Code Novel
by Rachel Van Dyken

SEDUCING MRS ROBINSON
Copyright © 2019 RACHEL VAN DYKEN
ISBN: 9781675880852
Editing by Kay Springsteen & Jill Sava
Cover Art by Jena Brignola
Formatting by Jill Sava, Love Affair With Fiction

To my son, Thor.
Happy fifth birthday buddy!
Enjoy it!
You aren't dating until you're forty!
I'm not kidding...

Prologue

"What's the opposite of a cougar?
Asking for a friend."
— Leo Blackwood

Leonardo Blackwood

High School Graduation 2013

"There she is." I elbowed my best friend in the ribs. "Kora Robinson." I made a sound of approval as she took the podium in a tight white dress that made me want to charge the stage and rip it off with my teeth.

She'd probably reprimand me for that.

And I'd probably enjoy it more than an eighteen-year-old should.

"Detention." I could see her perfect red pout forming the word.

Even the word got me hot and bothered after she spat it at me last time, with her bright red lipstick and less-than-amused pinch of a frown. It was her first year teaching, and technically she was only like eight years older.

Oh, also? She loathed me.

Like, she would drown me if she wouldn't get fired for it. Probably because I made her job a hell of a lot worse because I'm a flirt.

I can't apologize for it. I was born this way.

Honest to God, my mom said every single nurse in that delivery room was enamored, and well, here I am, breaking hearts at eighteen and making sure that older women know where the goods are because there really isn't anything better than a woman who knows her mind, her body, and how to use both to the best degree possible.

I gave a disgusted look across the auditorium at her new husband. It was all wrong. He was all wrong.

He was wearing thick black glasses that immediately made you think his dream was to live in a house that only used solar panels as its main source of energy. His jeans were skinny and tight, and he had no ass. His first mistake was skipping leg day, his second? Existing.

I snorted.

No biceps to speak of.

The white shirt was hanging loose off his thin-as-a-rail body, and I was pretty sure if I challenged him to a fight, he'd piss himself before actually answering with a sneer and saying something asinine such as real men used words like swords, not their fists.

God, I hated him.

The few times he'd stopped by the school to bring her lunch or visit, he never complimented her and always seemed to find something wrong with what she was wearing or how she did her hair. Which just provoked me to compliment

her on a daily basis, which then caused her to hate me even more because I was flirting twenty-four seven.

She kept making her speech, and dumb-ass kept texting on his phone like it wasn't a huge honor for her to be up there.

He was everything that was wrong with the world. Why the hell would a smoking hot woman like Mrs. Robison marry a guy who she could break in half? I mean, I guess he was hot in a rich nerd way?

And before you start getting pissed off about the personality being louder than the outside, well, he's a complete stuck up arrogant ass.

From money, loads of money, not that I was judging, I was from a wealthy family too, but this guy? He had a brand-new Tesla before the new model even came out and then got mad at her (slow your roll; I heard the argument in the parking lot, okay?) for driving it to work because her car had broken down.

Again.

See? Ass, total ass.

I shook my head in disgust for what had to have been the fifth time since she took the stage.

I couldn't take the look of boredom on his face as she started her speech about what a wonderful first year she'd had at West High.

Her voice was soft, and yet, she was still the loudest thing I heard in that gym. I crossed my arms over my chest and waited while the room erupted into applause, and then she turned to all three hundred of us and winked.

I wanted to believe that wink was for me.

It wasn't.

Because she followed it up with a scowl in my direction and because a man can't go against his true nature, I blew her a kiss. Ah yes, she wanted to strangle me alive.

Perfect. I would take hate over ignorance any day.

The rest of the day went by in a blur.

I talked with my friends.

I laughed about the summer before college.

I flirted with every able-bodied female who gave me attention—spoiler alert, I was the captain of the football team, so it was all of them. ALL of the women.

"Hey, you going to Mark's?" Eustice, horrible name, he's aware, jogged over to me and elbowed me in the side. His cap was off, and he'd already put on his typical black beanie, almost covering his eyes completely.

"Yeah, yeah," We were in the parking lot, sweating our balls off. "I'm just headed home to change real quick, then I'll meet you there. Sound good?"

"Yup." He waved me off with his middle finger.

I chuckled and made my way over to my new black Mercedes, a graduation gift from my parents.

They were givers.

They also wanted to make sure that straight A's were rewarded, I asked for a Benz when I was thirteen and kept my promise for five years. Thankfully my parents know me like they do a son because duh I'm their son and had already been looking for the safest, most badass car on the planet.

I had just unlocked the door when I heard yelling.

"I can't do this anymore!" Mrs. Robinson shouted. "I can't! It's not fair to me! I like my job!"

Oh, shit.

I looked over my shoulder. Sure enough, she was on the far side of the parking lot with her dick of a husband.

He leaned in and put his hands on her giving her a small shove.

Hard limit.

Hell no.

A man never puts his hands on a woman.

I was at their car in a minute, pulling him away from her within seconds. "Bro, I don't care how pissed you are, you don't touch a woman."

He tilted his head at me, his eyes feral. "Are you shitting me right now? What is this? Huh, Kora? You screwing a student now?"

"What?" I stepped between them. "Are you seriously that much of an idiot that you'd project your own insecurity in your manhood on your wife?"

He was silent, though a muscle popped in his jaw.

"Huh, guess you are. For your information, I have a girlfriend—actually several, not that it's any of your business. They like my dick since I actually have one... which is more than I can say about you, so back the hell off, cool down, and then have your very adult conversation— without laying a hand on your woman."

He sneered. "Last I checked she's not *your* wife."

"Last I checked, she's not a punching bag for you to toss around," I spat.

He paled and then looked like his body was convulsing with rage. Perfect. He jutted his finger at her. "This conversation isn't over. I'm going out with the guys tonight."

He got into his new car and sped off like I was chasing him, and I hoped to God that was the vision he had in his head, a high schooler, eight years his junior, scaring him so shitless he had to get in a car to get away.

Mrs. Robinson was pale, shaking. I towered over her, so I lowered my voice and asked as softly as I could, "Are you okay?"

"That wasn't your call to make!" Tears trailed down her puffy cheeks.

"Excuse me?" I reared back. "He was touching you! Hurting you!" I could see the fucking marks on her shoulder already, fingerprints, two of them. "He has no right to hurt you."

"He's my husband," she said softly.

"Then he should be the one protecting you." I gently touched her shoulder with my fingertips, and she winced. "Not the student you hate and wish you could have failed."

She looked away then, holding her purse strap so tight I was afraid she was going to pull the brown leather loose. "I gotta go."

"Mrs. Robinson." I grabbed her arm. Damn, it was soft. Her blue eyes pleaded with me, told me she needed me to stop talking, to stop touching, I was getting there, I just needed her to know. "A real man doesn't raise his voice at a woman, a real man doesn't touch a woman, a real man doesn't threaten a woman. I know I'm young, but I know what respect looks like, and this isn't it. If you need to talk to someone—"

"No." She pulled free, a sad smile on her face. "I'm fine, he's just stressed about some merger at work."

"Don't make excuses for the asshole."

She cleared her throat. "And don't touch your teachers without their permission, right?"

I felt deflated in that moment, the knight in shining armor being told the fair maiden never wanted saving from her own nightmare in the first place.

I nodded, and before I could stop myself before she closed the door to her car, I said, "You're one of the most beautiful women I have ever seen in real life, don't settle for a piece of shit just because he makes you think you have no other options." I pointed at myself. "Option number two." And then I turned and walked away.

Feeling like hell because I knew how their story would end.

In heartbreak.

Chapter One

"If she's moaning, but her pulse isn't erratic,
you're doing it wrong, bro, all wrong."
— Leo Blackwood

Leo

Present Day, Senior year at UW

"Right there, see that's better." I held Vanessa's delicate fingertips in mine and started slowly rubbing my thumb across the back of her hand. "Doesn't that feel better?"

Shoot me now.

She nodded tears in her eyes. "He never touched me like that."

"He wasn't good enough for you," I said it with such conviction, I knew she would walk away from this session feeling a million times better and most likely, finally, delete and block her ex's number from her phone.

He dumped her.

And it was my job as one part of the new Wingmen Inc to make sure that she felt aaallll better.

People called us the Pleasure Ponies. I had to admit the nickname kinda stuck, especially after it was rumored that visitors left our den of iniquity with such a relaxed smile on their faces that there was no way they didn't experience an orgasm.

The rumors grew and grew until it became such a thriving business on campus that we actually were getting to the point where we had to mentor some guys to take our spots once we graduated.

Knox, the leader of our group, was already working for Wingmen Inc downtown. The app was raking it in, and each of us had a position, if we wanted it, once we graduated.

At least then, I wouldn't be welcoming sad college students of both sexes into my dorm room in an effort to make them feel better about their lack of relationship prospects.

Vanessa straightened and gave me a shy smile. "You're really good at this, Leo."

Ah, I knew that smile.

"Don't confuse this," I whispered, "as anything but me helping you understand your own worth, all right? I don't date clients."

Her face fell. Ah, I knew that face well.

I was on the opposing end of that face, or had been, for four fucking years. Massive disappointment. Sorry not sorry. I really didn't have time for a relationship, especially since I had a full load this year right along with Wingmen work.

"But…" She licked her lips and leaned forward, placing both her hands on my denim-clad thighs. Huh, taught her that trick, quick learner. "Don't you think we'd be good together?"

I scooted my chair back and crossed my arms. "I'm gay."

She rolled her eyes. "You made out with Kelsie Garrett last year almost every single day of spring break…"

Damn it; I forgot we were all at Cabo together.

I cleared my throat. "Well, I could just like guys and girls. I'm kinda into both… maybe a little more dudes this semester, who knows?"

She narrowed her eyes. "Really?"

"Totally." I nodded solemnly. Hey, I appreciated the male form as much as anyone else! It wasn't a total lie! "I mean, have you seen the ass on Finn?"

Finn was my roommate, along with Slater, and all three of us made up the new and improved Pleasure Ponies.

Unfortunately, Finn chose that inopportune moment to open the door and grin down at Vanessa. "Hey sweetheart, how are you?"

I could practically feel the lust pulsing off her body. One of us was bad enough; both of us in the same room?

Clothes tended to just drop from people's bodies. It was a thing, involuntary, like breathing.

She pressed a hand to her chest and looked between us, "If you're into guys, I don't mind."

"Come again?" Finn asked, confused.

"We'll just add one more to the scenario." Damn, when had she gotten so brazen? She stood and pulled her shirt over her head.

And all my brain could conjure up was, boobs, nice boobs, boobs I'd like to touch, lick, maybe stick my—

"Whoa!" Slater walked in, took one look at her, looked at us, and just shook his head. "Yeah, Wingmen Inc doesn't really… cater to that sort of…" He gulped, looked his fill, even tilting his head to get a better angle, then murmured, "…thing."

"Really?" She grinned at him like she was seconds away from trapping him with her thighs and squeezing.

I could see his control slipping like a thousand pieces of sand through a baseball glove.

"All right then!" I grabbed her black tank off the floor, handed it to her, and then pointed her in the direction of the door. "We have another appointment. We'll make sure to charge this as your last session, and again, if you ever need anything from us, you know how to book through the online portal, mmkay?"

"You're missing out," she called after us.

"Totally," I agreed.

"Our loss," Slater added.

"You're so beautiful," Finn said just as the door shut, leaving her outside our dorm suite and us trapped on the inside. Great, just what I wanted this morning, to be surrounded by dudes all hot and bothered by a great set of tits.

"So… that went well," Finn finally said. His grin was maddening, one of those too-perfect things meant to disarm. With dimples, green eyes, and wavy dark hair, he looked like he belonged anywhere but a dorm room. The

guy could sell ice on the streets during a blizzard and make millions.

We each had our job.

I used my good looks and way with words to set the women at ease. Finn and Slater would simultaneously touch and show possession in a way that made the person feel loved and wanted, we were basically like a stand-in boyfriend to help you get through the rough patches after a breakup.

Someone should really give out badges for this shit.

I yawned, plopped back onto my bed, and grabbed my football. The one thing I missed. I had been here on scholarship—until I made a couple of poor life choices. But thankfully, the guys at Wingmen Inc saved me, grounded me with friendship, a purpose outside of sports, and, well, the rest was history. "You guys wanna go grab something to eat?"

"Can't." Slater grabbed the football midair and then chucked it at Finn's face. Finn, however, was used to the sneak attack and caught it one-handed, sending Slater an eye-roll. "I got class—wait, don't you have class too?"

I smirked. "Was thinking about skipping, I loathe my Senior Seminar."

"Really? Because I find it stimulating," Slater said in a bored tone.

I flipped him off and sat up. "Fine, I'll go to class, but only because you guys refuse to go grab food with me." My stomach rumbled on command.

"I can go after my lab." Slater shrugged. "We can meet later at the student union building?"

I gave him an incredulous look. "Right, because that wasn't a disaster last time all three of us decided to eat together. We were mauled by freshmen—BTS style!"

So what if we had a certain reputation on campus? It was almost like being famous without the money part. Then again, both me and Finn were loaded, and Slater? Well, he hid the fact that he had money very well, but we all knew who his father was; the guy wasn't fooling anyone, least of all us.

But we let him pretend.

"All right." I stood. "I'm out. I'll text you guys later, we'll go semi-off campus, so we don't come home with bras and thongs stuffed into our jeans."

"Worst day ever," Slater grumbled.

I just grinned, grabbed my shit, and shut the door behind me. Senior year; one more semester, and I was done.

Out of here.

Finally.

I kept a smug expression on my face as people whispered when I walked by. Some were brave enough to wave, others strategically took pictures with their phones.

It was a thing.

A thing I was finally used to after three years of putting up with it.

The business building wasn't necessarily close, but I needed the walk anyway, I hadn't worked out that day yet, and you don't get an eight-pack like mine without putting in at least two hours a day.

After around twenty minutes of speed walking, I finally made it to my building. Shit, I was going to be late. I took

the steps two at a time and at the top checked my phone, only to come to an abrupt halt when I collided with a warm body.

"Shit!" Papers went flying, a large black binder hit the ground along with two notebooks and several colored pens. I quickly bent over and grabbed the things I could reach. "You know, they have bags for this kind of stuff..."

"Sarcasm, how shocking to find that in a college student." The warm voice wrapped around me.

I froze and slowly looked up.

And there she was.

Woman of my dreams... or at least several schoolboy fantasies.

Mrs. Robinson.

My grin grew. "Well, well, well, what do we have here?"

Her eyes narrowed. "*We* have nothing," She jerked her stuff away from my hands and stood. "You should really watch where you're going."

"I was texting and walking, a crime punishable by kiss..." I winked. "Wait, I think I got that wrong."

"Ah, so you've lost more brain cells since graduation, how sad." Her stony glare was doing nothing to deter me. "Now, if you'll excuse me, I'm late."

She was wearing her light brown hair in a tight bun, had diamond studs in her ears, and if her black dress were any more boring, I would say she looked like she was headed to the nunnery or at the very least a funeral.

Hah, mine probably.

I reached out and touched her shoulder, just light enough for her to look at my fingertips and then my face.

It always worked; it was the point where the female realized that my touch was commanding, warm, and oh so very promising.

My favorite part.

The soft intake of breath she sucked through her mouth.

The way her eyes tried to focus on anything but mine and failed miserably.

"See something you like, Mrs. Robinson?" I whispered it low, so only she could hear me.

She jerked back like she'd been electrocuted and scowled. "Like I said, I'm late, and you have something on your face."

"No, I don't," I said smugly.

"You do." She turned on her heel and marched off.

And because I was just that vain, I quickly checked my selfie mode on my phone just to make sure she was wrong and was relieved to find out that she had needed an escape.

From me.

It had been four years.

She looked like she needed a good orgasm—or seven.

And I was only too happy to volunteer.

I smiled the entire way to my class, jerked open that door with a stupid grin on my face, only to look at the front of the room and see Mrs. Robinson standing where our professor should be standing.

"Mrs. Cordy went into labor, so I'll be your adjunct professor for the rest of the year while she takes her maternity leave." She smiled warmly at the class, nearly knocking me on my ass. Damn, she was beautiful. "Mr. Blackwood, is this going to be a habit for you?

"Smiling?" I offered, slowly making my way to the first available seat, noticing all the girls fanning themselves as I passed them.

I really couldn't help it.

"Being tardy," she said through clenched teeth while I sat and put my hands behind my neck, giving her a full view of my massive body.

Pink flushed her cheeks while she waited for my answer.

"That's one thing you'll never have to worry about with me, Mrs. Robinson," I said her name with reverence. "I'm very punctual in all areas of my life, physical, mental, educational..." I gave her a confident grin. "Any self-respecting man knows that it's always important to show up on time—you never know what you could miss, maybe even a blast from the past..." I cleared my throat and flippantly waved my hand. "For example."

"Right." She dropped a book onto her desk and gave me an annoyed grin. "Let's hope you're not just talking out of your—"

I waited.

Silence fell.

"My what?"

She clenched her teeth. "Nothing."

The class snickered.

"All right, now that we have that settled." She pasted another fake smile on her face. "Let's talk about your senior projects..."

I heard nothing the rest of class.

I did, however, take notes on every single movement she

made, from the way she addressed the class, to the way she seemed to hide behind her ugly as fuck black dress.

Ninety minutes later, I decided she needed me.

I waited for everyone to leave and, still sitting at my table, raised my hand.

She rolled her eyes. "I have another class."

"And I have a question."

"Fine, what's your question?" She crossed her arms and leaned back against the desk.

I stood and slowly made my way across the room to her, towering over her in a way that made her seem to shrink into herself. Instinct told me to pull her into my arms, but my brain reminded me she'd probably knee me in the balls, so I refrained.

"My question…" I searched her eyes. "It's more of an observation, I guess."

She gulped. "And?"

"You're sexually repressed."

"Excuse me?" She looked ready to murder me on the spot.

I just grinned and gestured toward her left hand. "No wedding ring."

"I have a boyfriend."

"Then he's clearly doing it wrong," I fired back and then lowered my gaze to her clenched fists. "All fucking wrong."

"Language."

I pressed my lips together in a smile. "You're not offended. In fact, by the blush I see on your cheeks, you're both intrigued and aroused. Trust me, I know my women."

"Ah, so you decided to grow up and become a manwhore? Pimp? Which is it? Both?"

I burst out laughing. "Oh, sweetheart, none of the above... Some might say I'm their worst nightmare dressed as a daydream."

"Did you just quote Taylor Swift?"

"So what? She has catchy lyrics." I chuckled. "Ask around about me, if you're that curious. Just know, I could make all of this—" I pointed at her. "—feel like an old school Herbal Essences commercial with more moaning and at least ten more minutes of shower time."

Her expression was unreadable. And then finally she sighed. "Not interested."

"Liar... By the way, how's the ex-husband? Rotting in Hell? If not, I'll add in a little voodoo doll and give you the pins. Works every time."

"You charge extra for that?"

"What makes you think I'd charge you at all?" I countered.

"So, you *are* a pimp?"

"Nope." People started shuffling in, I slowly backed away and locked eyes with her. "Thanks for the help... Mrs. Robinson..."

"Yeah." Her voice was hollow, her expression a bit unnerved, her cheeks still rosy from our conversation.

She didn't know.

I had her right where I wanted her.

Chapter Two

"I've always had a thing for librarians.
Nothing hotter than a pair of spectacles and a face that says
I'll spank you later."
— Leo Blackwood

Kora

Later, in my office, I seethed. I was going to murder him with my bare hands. It had been at least two years since I'd felt such rage directed at the opposite sex.

Who knew it would be directed at Leo Blackwood, of all people! He just had to attend this specific university? I dug into my lame turkey sandwich with fervor.

I'd been able to distract myself with class all day, but now that I was alone eating dinner behind my new desk, I couldn't escape the memories of his smoldering looks or the brazen way he'd talked to me with suggestively charged references to moaning and shower time. Didn't he realize that a university had rules about this sort of thing? Granted, I hadn't actually seen the rule book, but they had to have some clause about professors and students.

Not that I was interested.

Not at all.

I mean, it was laughable.

I bit my tongue and dropped my sandwich onto the Ziplock bag in front of me then reached for my Diet Coke.

The audacity of that boy.

Boy, hah, he was anything but.

He was six feet five inches of pure masculine godlike beauty, all wrapped up in a pretty package with wavy golden hair, deep green eyes, and a tendency to smirk way too often.

Heck, he'd had a killer smirk back in high school. There had been no escaping his good looks even then. He was just this massive presence that refused to be ignored, like a hot teddy bear.

I shuddered. Bad example.

He'd stood up for me when my ex was being condescending again. I was so embarrassed that an eighteen-year-old student had to be the one to tell my husband at the time to stop touching me.

And sadly, things had gotten worse soon after.

I wrapped my arms around my middle and held myself still, trying to just breathe in and out, but nothing was really helping the rising panic or the bile in my throat.

He wasn't here.

He wasn't in my life anymore.

I stared at the small sandwich in front of me and tried to focus on the positive. I had a new job that would help me possibly get tenure at UW if I played my cards right. I had no debt to speak of or wouldn't once my ex paid out what I was due.

And I was happy.

So. Happy.

My thoughts went back to Leo, smirking Leo.

How dare he assume I would even want to start up with someone seven years younger than me!

His arrogance was borderline insulting.

I managed to take another small bite of my sandwich and turned toward my computer just in time to see a little email pop up.

From the devil himself.

> *Dear Mrs. Robinson,*
>
> *I've been having some trouble with deciding the topic of my Senior Project, can you please send me a copy of your office hours so you can make yourself available to a star student?*
>
> *Regards,*
>
> *Leo*

I wanted to reply with irritation, but this was my university employee email. And he wasn't technically out of bounds asking for my office hours. I just knew he had ulterior motives.

With a sigh, I typed a response.

> *Dear Star Student,*
>
> *I regret to inform you that I must remove said star before your name as every single person in my class has already chosen a topic—meaning you're the last to decide*

what your senior project should be on. That doesn't speak of stardom but laziness. My office hours are every afternoon from one to five, though I'm not sure I can help motivate you—I can give you a list of topics that would be appropriate.

Sincerely,

PROFESSOR ROBINSON

The all caps probably weren't necessary, but I had no other choice. He needed to be reminded who I was, how old I was, just… everything.

I reached for my sandwich and continued eating, hating myself that I was disappointed that he wasn't hovering over his laptop or phone, ready to email me back right away.

I was just about to take another bite when there was a soft knock on my door. A glance toward the sound revealed Leo lounging against the jamb. I started choking on my bite, tears filling my eyes.

And Leo, with his superhero complex fully intact, rushed over to my chair, pulled me to my feet, and started doing the Heimlich.

A piece of food went flying out of my mouth and onto the floor. His arms were still around me. And I prayed for death.

Because, why? Why did bad things always have to happen to me?

"You okay?" He rasped in my right ear.

I could feel the heat of his breath, and of course, he had minty breath because this was Leo we were talking about; he probably had a huge dick too.

Shit!

I needed therapy.

I quickly pulled away and smoothed my hands down my black dress. It was ugly, but it did its job—repel everything except the unlucky gaze of the one that needed to be repelled the most.

"Thank you." I managed to get the words out and put a chair between us. "I'm assuming you're here for the senior project topics?"

"Sure." He crossed his arms. "Because why else would I be visiting your office at four in the afternoon, by myself, where most of the professors have already gone home because… Friday."

My eyes narrowed. "Leo, I think you have the wrong impression here."

"No." He said confidently. "Don't think so."

I gritted my teeth and tried a different tactic. Ignorance. "Fine, let me grab you a sheet, it has topics past Seniors have done their projects on. You're already behind, so I'd hop to it."

"Did you just say hop to it?" He grinned.

No. "Yup." So, just… "Shoo."

Could I sound any more like my grandma?

Probably not.

I inwardly winced as his expression turned from amused to dark, threatening. I moved farther back. I knew that look. I'd seen it countless times on my ex-husband. Panic made me freeze as I closed my eyes and flinched, then opened them as he neared. He lifted his hand. Oh God, it was happening again—

And brushed my cheek with his fingertips.

I trembled waiting for what might happen next.

"You had a crumb," he whispered and then added, "And a woman should never flinch in front of a man. That tells me one thing. Your ex-husband is a complete asshole who should burn in Hell."

He said it so softly but with such ferocity all at once.

I opened my eyes. He was staring at me like he wanted to take away all the bad, and part of me believed he probably could.

Or that if anyone could—it would be Leo Blackwood.

The teen I wasn't supposed to find attractive my first year of teaching.

The teen who flirted with me for nine blissful months.

The teen who made me wonder what it would feel like if we had just one wild night.

That was then.

This is now.

"Mrs. Robinson?" Another voice broke into my thoughts, one of my sophomore girls stood in the doorway. She'd asked about a billion questions during Intro to Business Marketing. "Sorry if you're busy I can come back."

"No, Sheila, we were finished." I grinned at her. "Leo, make sure you look over the worksheet and let me know if you have any questions."

"Oh, I'll have questions." He winked and walked by Sheila without even making eye contact.

Huh, so he did have asshole tendencies.

"OMG!" Sheila shut the door and leaned against it. "I

cannot believe you had Leo Blackwood in your office, and you're still standing!"

"I'm sorry, why wouldn't I be standing?"

Her eyes widened. "Last year a girl said she had an orgasm watching him eat Lucky Charms." She paused dramatically, then whispered. "I believe her."

I burst out laughing. "That's ridiculous and semi-inappropriate to discuss."

"It's true! The guys from Wingmen Inc are notorious around campus."

"Wait, Wingmen Inc?" I repeated. "The dating app that's worth a billion dollars and nestled nicely next to the Amazon campus in downtown Seattle?"

"Uh-huh," She pulled out a chair like this explanation was going to take a while. "So, the main guys Ian and Lex wanted to leave a presence on campus, and they handpicked four guys. Knox graduated last year, and the other three are rounded out by Leo, Slater, and Finn. They make girls and guys, plants, grandmas, whomever—rediscover their worth and sexuality. Oh, and if you go through a shitty breakup, they'll make you feel better... for a price."

"Wait." It was too ridiculous to even process. "What do you mean for a price?"

She held up a finger and tapped away at her iPhone then turned the screen toward me.

WingmenIncUniversity.com.

And there he was, shirtless.

"Having a bad breakup? Are you sad? Are you nervous for your first date? Or do you just need someone to tell you how incredible you are? Look no further! Sign up for a time slot today! Discounts for people who schedule out more than five sessions. We'll make you feel all better. Wingmen Inc. You're welcome."

My jaw dropped. "Is this legal?"

"Duh, they've been featured on The Today Show like twice. Of course, it's legal. Nothing overtly sexual ever happens. That's in their little—" she wiggled her fingers, making air quotes "—'rule book.' It's like they know magical ways to make energy fields explode around a person's body. This one time…"

She went on and on for another hour.

And I sat there slack-jawed, too intrigued to stop her.

"…And her grandma said that she felt her husband's spirit when Leo touched her… and he *barely* touched her. Then his lips grazed her ear, and she cried. Oh, oh, and one time, Slater was doing laundry, and a girl was a total train wreck in the laundry room because her boyfriend had cheated on her. Well, ten minutes with Slater and I've never seen a person smile so big in my entire life. People jokingly call them the Pleasure Ponies, but I believe it, I mean I've been with my boyfriend for two years, but I would drop him in a second for a chance to date one of those guys…"

My head whipped up. "Wait, they don't date?"

"No, it's in the rules. They can't date paying clients, and it's frowned upon to date at all when you're working for Wingmen at their level. They're all promised a job at Wingmen Corporate when they graduate, not that Leo needs it since he's independently wealthy…"

"His parents, you mean." I corrected her.

She gave me a funny look. "No, Leo. The guys all get a

percentage of the profits, and when they send people to the app, they get a royalty. Trust me, everyone wants that job. Plus, Leo's brilliant. Word on the street is he's worth over eight million because of the way he's invested his earnings, but who knows, it could be inflated. Nobody's sure about that."

I was dumbfounded.

Completely speechless.

"Isn't he only twenty-one?"

"Twenty-two." She grinned. "He had a birthday last week. It was the party of the year."

"I bet it was."

"So," Sheila yawned. "Wow, I forgot why I was even here." She stood, and I handed her phone back. "Oh, I remember, can I have another outline from Marketing? I lost mine, and I really want to ace this class."

"Sure." I was still processing everything she'd said hours later when I was home alone in my two-bedroom apartment overlooking the sound.

And like someone obsessed, I grabbed my laptop and started to find out everything I could about Wingmen Inc's lucrative business dealings on campus, mainly… those of one Leo Blackwood.

Chapter Three

"Flirting is the best kind of foreplay. Find a way to make them think about you when they don't want to, and they'll spend way too much time trying not to think about you. See also: Winning, folks."
— *Leo Blackwood*

Leo

"*Y*ou look tense." Slater elbowed Finn, causing his tomatoes to fall from his hamburger. "Doesn't he look tense?"

"You ruined my favorite part." He glared at Slater then back down at his food.

I made a face. "The tomato should never be the favorite part, especially if it's too moist."

"Why, God, why?" Slater grumbled. "Why ruin food for us? You know that word triggers me!"

"Everything triggers you." Finn snorted.

"Bullshit!" Slater took a huge mouthful of fries.

"Oh, he wants a list," Finn said to himself and then nodded to me as I held up one finger.

"Hair. you hate hair on bodies, hair in the shower, hair on the floor, hell you probably pluck your own eyelashes you know that's a psychological condition caused by stress?"

Finn held out his hand for a high five then held up two fingers. "Last year you were triggered by a crumb."

Slater glared. "For your information, one of my best friends back home nearly died from a crumb, he made his sandwich next to it and bam, rat poison!"

"First of all," I laughed. "Your best friend's an idiot, you never make a fresh sandwich on crumbs, second, he's an idiot."

"True." Finn tore into his burger just as I held up three fingers.

"Oh, dear God." Slater shoved his food back. "Fine, fine, I'm more... sensitive than others."

"Be honest man." I winked. "Do your own jeans turn you on? I've always wanted to know, not because I'm even minutely interested in the way you get off, but I have never seen a dude so physically and emotionally sensitive."

"Right?" Finn looked between us and then under the table.

Slater gave us both the finger. "Don't be jealous. The ladies love it, and for your information no, my zipper doesn't get me off, though I wouldn't complain if I just had multiple orgasms every time I—" He winced. "—no that's a lie, I wouldn't want that, I saw something like that on Grey's Anatomy. Looked painful as hell, not to mention loud. I mean, can you imagine?"

I threw my head back and made a face then slammed my hands onto the table. "Yessss, oh God, yessss!"

Finn threw a fry at my face.

I opened my eyes and laughed.

"What the hell was that?" Slater gaped.

"Your orgasm face," Finn answered for me as I held up my hand for a high five.

"Sometimes, I hate you guys." Slater shook his head and laughed.

We joined in, and then Finn tilted his head toward me. "Hey, what's my face look like?"

"Yeah, you don't want to know," said Slater.

I nodded.

More fries got thrown. I ate a few and then confessed, "I have a mad crush on my new professor. She was one of my teachers, senior year of high school, married to a complete douche, and now she's divorced and looking every inch the uptight librarian he probably wanted her to be." I sighed and scooted my food away, appetite gone.

"Tight bun?" Slater asked.

"Yup."

"Dark clothing?" Finn guessed.

"Yup."

"Permanent scowl that looks painful?" Slater again.

"What do you think?" I snorted.

"What about her skin? Moisturized?" Finn leaned in.

I narrowed my eyes. "How the hell would I know?"

"It's a thing." He shrugged. "If a woman still cares about basic needs like skincare, oral hygiene, shaving—she still cares, get it?"

Slater nodded slowly. "Teach us, oh wise one."

"Soon grasshopper." Finn bowed. "Soon."

I rolled my eyes and blew out a frustrated breath. "Well, unless I can somehow get her to become a client, it's hands-off and even then… I don't want you two dipshits anywhere near her."

"He's scared of a little challenge." Slater stretched his arms overhead.

"Yes, little," I pointed at his dick, "is absolutely correct."

Slater cackled out a laugh. "Hey, if lying makes you feel better."

"Hmm." Finn seemed to be thinking way too hard about something I'd already spent the last few hours thinking about. "You could always pull a friend zone?"

"Bite your tongue!" I hissed. "Are you insane?"

"He's right." Slater shrugged and pointed at my half-eaten burger. "You gonna finish that?"

I shoved the basket toward him and threw my hands up in the air toward Finn. "I'm not purposely shooting myself in the kneecaps over this one."

"Your arrogance won't win this one, Leo." Finn shrugged. "If she's been hurt and she's all tightly bound, you can't just force yourself. She'll run away. But you can slowly and surely un-peel the damaged layers, as a friend, and then take the chance that you send her into someone else's arms."

"Leaving me miserable and alone?" I sighed. "Awesome plan. Where do I sign up?"

"And there it is," Slater said, mouth full of food. "You want to settle down. I knew I saw the itch on your face this year. Look, all you gotta do is tell Ian and Lex that you're hitting retirement early from the business. They couldn't care less. We'll just keep recruiting."

"So, that's it?" I asked, more to myself than anything. "I friend zone her, take a chance she actually wants me for more than that, and then what? Retire and live happily ever after working at corporate?"

"Pretty much." Finn smiled wide.

"Maybe you'll get lucky, and I'll sing at your wedding." Slater laughed.

I didn't join in.

Because panic was too busy spreading through my chest, down my arms and legs.

Was it that easy?

And why the hell was my heart beating so hard at the thought of dating a woman who didn't want me?

I loved my job for the campus Wingmen.

Settling down.

Huh.

"I'll need to think about it," I whispered.

"We'll be here when you need to strategize." Slater nodded. "Because you've never been the friend zone, that's all Finn and me. It's like you can't help but hit on anything that breathes."

I shrugged. "It's a gift."

"That she'll return," Finn said slowly.

"Fine," I snapped. "Let me just… do some recon."

"He's so romantic." Slater snorted.

"I damn near swooned," Finn agreed.

"You dicks are paying." I stood and made my way over to the bathroom just in time to see Mrs. Robinson walk into the restaurant, take one good look at me, and walk right back out.

Well, shit.

Chapter Four

"Make it impossible for them not to notice you.
If necessary, be shirtless."
— *Leo Blackwood*

Kora

He was everywhere.

It wasn't fair. He'd even managed to take over my favorite Starbucks down the street from my apartment, though he seemed to be in heavy conversation with someone else almost equally as good looking.

They had charts and a laser pointer.

I'd slowly backed away and gone to Peet's instead. Not my first choice.

It had officially been two weeks since that fateful day in my office, and he'd been nothing but polite since then.

If polite meant he smiled at me constantly, offered to carry my books, and left an apple on my desk like a fifth-grader.

Maybe I was the stupid one because I bit into that apple

every break with trembling fingertips and a little heat in my face.

If an apple can do that, imagine.

Just. Imagine.

Maybe my other student had it right when she said a girl had orgasmed watching him eat Lucky Charms.

Lucky bitch.

I managed to make it into my office that Friday without running into him and was weirdly disappointed when Leo's face wasn't looking back at me before office hours.

My hand even felt the lack of apple.

Maybe that was part of his plan.

Drive me crazy over free fruit until I lose my mind and just maul him instead.

I smirked and dropped my messenger bag on the chair just in time for my phone to buzz in my purse.

I stared down at the screen and felt my stomach plummet. The caller ID said Satan.

It was him. My sorry excuse for an ex.

I quickly hit decline and dropped the phone onto my desk with a bang.

What could he possibly want?

He'd gotten more and more aggressive ever since the divorce, to the point that I thought I was going to need a restraining order—and then he'd just stopped. It was like he wasn't happy unless he was making someone else miserable and small. It was the main reason I moved farther into the city and left my job—it was far, far, away from Issaquah, where we'd both lived during those first few years of marriage.

My body gave an involuntary shudder as I thought about those dark times. Times where he would yell for no reason, where he would grab my arm too hard, make me flinch like he was going to hit me.

And then one day he had.

He'd hit me.

And Leo's words came back to haunt me.

I wasn't sure who I hated more. My husband, myself, or Leo for knowing even then.

I opened my laptop and started checking emails at about the same time something rolled by my feet.

I gave a start, cringed, and then looked down.

It was a red apple.

With a swift intake of breath, I turned toward the door.

Nobody was there? At least not anymore.

I picked it up and written in permanent marker across the red skin was, "An apple a day keeps a Leo at bay."

Huh? Did that mean that if I didn't get apples anymore, he'd suddenly show up? And why did that make my heart pick up speed?

Student. Student. Student.

I quickly got up and looked down the hall.

He wasn't there anymore.

But now he was all I could think about again.

This had to be some sort of game to him.

See if he could sleep with the professor. I exhaled and walked back to my desk and quickly pulled up Wingmen Inc University.

Naturally, Leo's picture was front and center with two other guys who looked like they should be in modeling campaigns, the same guys at Starbucks earlier. No wonder people went crazy over them.

I scrolled down.

"Ex do a number on you? We're only a phone call away! Bonus, we won't dump you because we can't date clients! Besides, sometimes having someone tell you how awesome you are without wanting something in return is kinda nice. No lies. Only truth. Who are we? Wingmen Inc!"

I quickly clicked out of the website and stared at my screen saver. It was a picture of my cat and me.

Ugh.

Could I be any more lame?

Stuart was the only good thing about my scary relationship. I'd always wanted a pet, and my ex had been allergic to all things, so I'd decided to buy a naked cat. The only problem was that it was hard to find a cat sitter.

Apparently, naked cats are gross?

Who knew?

I drummed my fingertips on my desk, my thoughts going back to Leo and Wingmen.

And five hours later, when I was back at my apartment, my phone rang again.

What could he possibly want?

I finally answered. "Yes?"

"Been calling you all day," Chadwick barked. "Why didn't you answer?"

I officially hated my ex. "I was working, making money so I can live in my apartment and afford to feed myself."

"Ungrateful bitch, it's not like you aren't going to take half."

This again. "I told you I don't want anything."

"Yeah. Right." He muttered something under his breath. "Look, I have a wedding I need to go to, family thing. It's in two weeks. Can you make it?"

I frowned hard, stared at my phone then spoke into it. "Chadwick, we're divorced. Why would I go with you?"

"Separated."

And there it was. My stomach dropped like a lead ball. "You promised you signed the papers last month."

"Been busy."

I squeezed my eyes shut as fresh tears built, threatening to roll down my cheeks. I was so damn sick of his games. "Right."

"Look, go with me to the wedding, I'll personally hand you the paperwork once we're done, and you'll make Mom happy."

He sounded like the old Chadwick, but I knew he was a narcissist to the extreme. Things were always my fault even when they were his, and he would do whatever it took to come out of this looking like a victim.

"I'll think about it," I found myself saying.

"Do that. And I'll do the same about the papers." The line went dead.

I let out a scream and charged into my kitchen, opened a bottle of wine, and went to town.

It was after the first glass that I found my laptop open again.

The website from before taunted me.

And two hours after that, I'd done the unthinkable.

With Stuart in my lap and most of the wine gone, I filled out the application and hit *send* along with my first payment.

And promptly fell asleep.

Cheers.

Chapter Five

*"The friend zone is just another way to say
that the woman of your dreams thinks of you
the same fucking way she does her golden retriever.
See also: Frigid and sexually repugnant."*
— Leo Blackwood

Leo

*O*peration Seducing Mrs. Robison by way of friendship was underway, and so far I was ready to drown my sorrows in alcohol and a shit ton of weed—hey don't judge it's legal in Washington, not that I've even gone out of my way to buy any because I hate the way it feels.

But right now? I could use something.

Anything.

Fifteen red apples.

One with a note on it yesterday.

Several smiles and friendly hellos.

And she still narrowed her eyes at me like I was a math problem she needed to figure out so she could get rid of me for good and store me in the solved part of her brain.

I lay down on my bed, only to have my door burst open with Slater and Finn on the other side, shit-eating grins on their faces.

"Day drinking?" I asked casually.

"Wait for it." Slater held out his laptop and turned it toward me.

I frowned as my eyes took in the new contact form, and then I nearly shit my pants when I saw the name.

Kora Fucking Robinson.

"What the hell!" I roared, nearly tripping over my duvet as I got to my feet. "She just magically signed up?"

"Came in at one a.m." Finn grinned. "So, I'm thinking alcohol was involved, bonus for you now she has no choice but to be around you."

I gritted my teeth. "Perfect! You do realize this means my entire plan goes to hell, right? I can't date her, I can't seduce her, I can't even really be her friend in this scenario. Hell, I can't be your friends in this scenario because I'll be too busy murdering you for touching her."

"He really likes her." Finn held up his hand to Slater.

They high fived over my pain.

Assholes!

"Look." Slater put his hand on my shoulder. "I know manwhores like yourself struggle to understand the concept of friendship, so let's start with something you do understand. Time."

"Time," I repeated.

"Time," they said in unison.

I rolled my eyes. "Why are we talking about time? Are

we going back in time to prevent her from signing up so I can swoop in?"

"Swoop in… nice." Slater grunted. "Like you're going to eat her."

I grinned. "Well—"

"Don't." Finn shook his head. "We can finish that sentence all by ourselves, thanks."

Slater set down the computer and braced me with both of his hands. "The first appointment is always an hour, an hour where you get to sit with her, learn about her likes and dislikes, compliment her. Use the time you've been given because she's not going to be a client forever, and the sooner you help her heal over whatever the hell she's struggling with, the sooner she drops Wingmen, and then you can do your swooping."

"I want to swoop now," I grumbled.

"You would probably miss and land on your ass, just saying," Finn said helpfully.

"Thanks." I clenched my jaw. "All right, when are you scheduling her?"

"Two hours from now." Finn rocked back on his heels. "So, you better bring your A-game."

"Great." I sighed. "And I get to do all of this with you two. Just what I wanted, to watch you touch her while I try to find out a way to date her."

"We'll be gentle." Slater winked.

"This is so messed up." I tugged my hair. "Fine, fine, but don't go all pleasure pony on her, all right? None of that Reiki shit either, Finn, I mean it! The last girl orgasmed."

"I set her free." Finn shrugged.

My. Ass. He'd learned that gift of massage without touching way too quickly, and there was no chance in hell I wanted him near her.

"Do you hear yourself?" I asked. "I'm genuinely curious?"

"He's not wrong," Slater added.

"Aghhhhhhhhhhh." I banged my head against the door. "No oils, no candles, no—"

"Bro." Slater shoved me away from the door and opened it. "We know how to do our jobs. Go take a shower, so you don't smell like pickles, and we'll get everything ready."

"I don't smell like pickles," I protested under my breath.

"Yeah, okay big guy." Another shove from Slater.

"I like pickles, though," I muttered.

"Nobody said they were bad," Finn said helpfully. "Go shower, do all the things, and try not to panic."

"Don't panic," I repeated. "Don't. Panic." I took a step toward the common area. "I'm not panicking. I mean, how bad could it really be?"

They wisely chose not to answer.

Meaning I had my answer.

It was going to be a living Hell.

Chapter Six

"My smile should make you think of every dirty fantasy you've ever had. My secret? It's all in the side smile. I call it the Leo face, and yes, it works ninety-nine percent of the time. Wingmen Inc tested and approved."
— *Leo Blackwood*

Kora

I woke up with a splitting headache and a vague memory of applying to the campus Wingmen.

And when I checked my phone, my nightmare just kept happening. It was from a subscription number, and it said: "Congrats! We're so excited to meet your needs this afternoon at three p.m. Wear something comfortable and don't be nervous. Not only are we as professional as they come—but you'll walk away feeling like you've just been set free."

I gaped at the message.

Did people really buy that crap?

"Aghhhhh." I slammed a pillow over my face and felt

a paw on my thigh. Stuart made his way into my lap and snuggled.

I was doing this.

If for no other reason than I got drunk with my cat last night.

Alone.

In my apartment.

I cringed.

When had I turned into that woman? The one who hid away from the world? Had Chadwick morphed me into that, or was it the only way to protect myself from him? From others?

I worried my lower lip and stood on wobbly legs. I had three classes to teach, and then apparently—I was going to get my life changed by way of three college Co-Ed's who apparently knew how to give orgasms without touching.

I wasn't sure if I should be horrified or excited.

I took one look in the mirror. My cheeks were flushed, my hair was a mess around my face. Horrified. Definitely horrified.

The day went by fast. Thankfully I didn't have Leo in any of my classes, though I was cursed to have one of the other guys in my last class. He was too gorgeous for words and kept smiling as if we shared a secret. He didn't leer; he just… looked excited? Was that right?

"So." I cleared my throat, ready to dismiss the class and

head over to my appointment. "If anyone has any questions, you can email me over the weekend. Class dismissed."

Everyone shuffled out, the sound of people making plans almost depressed me more. The only plan I had was to go meet with a few guys younger than me and hope to feel better, and the only reason I was even going through with it is because I know Leo would give me hell if I chickened out. Well, that and I was curious.

And lonely.

And sad.

Damn it!

"Hey." Finn moved in front of my line of vision. His smile was friendly, open. His brownish blond hair was tucked under a black beanie, and his green eyes sparkled with mischief. His poor mother.

I bet she used prayer beads on a daily basis in hopes he didn't give people heart attacks simply by existing.

"Hey." I managed to find my voice; it sounded like I was giving birth to a hyena.

He jerked his head toward the door. "I know you have a few minutes until your next appointment. I figured it might calm your nerves if I walk with you, answer some questions if you have any."

I exhaled and nodded. "Yeah, actually, that would be nice. It was an impulse, you know."

He smirked knowingly. "Always is."

"I mean, signing up. I may have had a bit too much wine and—"

He pressed a finger to my lips and winked. "I'm not a priest, no need for confessions here, sweetheart. I promise whatever you need, we can provide it, though I'm pretty sure Leo's heart may not handle anyone else touching you."

I frowned. "The player has a heart?"

"Terrifying, am I right?" He flicked off the room's lights and opened the door, letting me go out first.

"Absolutely."

He had his hand on the small of my back as he opened the door again, and I almost didn't walk through it, not because I was being a chicken but because I couldn't remember the last time Chadwick had opened a door for me.

And for some stupid reason, I felt like crying. My throat was thick with emotion as I slowly stepped through the door.

"He's right," Finn whispered.

"What? Who?" I forced a smile.

"Leo." He sighed. "Your ex is an asshole."

I barked out a laugh. "Yeah, pretty much."

"I have a friend, you know, pretty high up in the mafia, just say the words and—" He made an exploding motion with his hands.

I laughed.

He didn't.

I sobered. "No need for violence."

"It's not violent if he doesn't feel a thing." He just shrugged and kept walking. "So, Leo's going to be doing the actual intake while we use sock puppets and charts—"

"What?"

He burst out laughing. "I'm kidding. Well, not about the intake, but no sock puppets, no puppets at all, no

charts, no whips, no chains, and I truly have no idea how the whole Lucky Charms rumor even got started. It's been disproven many times."

"How disappointing." I joked.

He flashed me a grin. "Careful, or I might throw my hat in."

"Hat in?"

"The ring, see only one of us gets to kiss you on the mouth, and I'm pretty sure I could get yours to say some pretty wicked things."

My cheeks heated. "I thought—"

"You'll see." He chuckled. "Anything you're curious about?"

"Um, well…" We started walking toward what I liked to call the nice new dorms. Each had a common area shared between the rooms, with fully stocked fridges, pantries. It was basically for the rich kids and athletes, not that the administration would ever admit it. "Do I get a safe word?"

He smiled. "You won't need that, Kora, because you'll be safe the entire time, and why the hell would you need a word other than 'stop'?"

I tilted my head. "You seem older than a senior in college."

Something flashed in his eyes. "Yeah, well, they don't pick us just because we're pretty, and that's all I'm going to say about that."

I touched his arm, not sure why. We both stopped walking. "If you need to talk."

"You gonna be my therapist?" he fired back softly, his eyes darting from my mouth back up to my face. "Don't worry, I'm all better, but just because I'm functioning doesn't mean the scars don't still pull, you know what I mean?"

"Yeah." I sighed. "I really do."

"That's why I like my job." He opened the door to the dorm and ushered me in. "I get to help people, I get to make them realize their own potential, there's nothing in it for me other than giving something to someone who needs it. When someone's hungry, you give them food, but when you're emotionally starved, it's hard to see where the need is. That—" he pressed the elevator button "—is Wingmen Inc."

"That's deep." I stepped inside.

"Don't be fooled by the player facades, Kora. Each of us plays a part in a multimillion-dollar business here on campus. And we're fucking good at our jobs. Remember that when you see Leo tonight."

I gulped. "Okay."

"And here we are." We stepped off the elevator and turned the corner, they were in a suite. Of course they were. He opened the door, and I was instantly hit with the warm smell of cinnamon and something else… chocolate maybe?

Two bottles of wine sat on the main table—one in ice and the other breathing—an assortment of chocolates was on a nice plate, and soft music played in the background.

I let out a little gasp when Leo stepped out of the bedroom in nothing but low-slung jeans and a smile. "Ready?"

Abs. So many abs I got dizzy.

"Close your mouth." Finn coughed under his breath.

Another guy stood behind Leo. Slater, I remembered

from the website. He was a bit leaner, with darker skin, and then Finn turned to me and peeled off his shirt. "Let's do this."

"Am I shirtless too?" I asked, dumbfounded.

"Not unless you wanna be, sweetheart," Finn joked, at least I think he was joking. "And most of our clients stay completely clothed, easier for us to focus that way."

"Yeah, except Grandma Jean," Leo said in a totally serious voice.

"Grandma?" I squeaked.

"We don't discriminate." Leo winked. "Let's go, Kora, time to feel better."

My heart beat out of my chest as I took five steps toward him, and then I was inside his room, and someone was asking me what sort of wine I preferred.

And then Leo's gorgeous green eyes locked on mine, and I knew.

I was better.

Just because I was sitting across from him.

Chapter Seven

*"There is nothing sexier than a woman who owns her body
and makes no apologies for the battle scars she's survived to get
to where she is. Show me a scar over tits any day—
because it's all about the story, isn't it?"*
— Leo Blackwood

Leo

I was sweating bullets. Why the hell hadn't I turned on
the AC? She looked so prim and proper sitting there,
her lips parted just enough for me to want to tease them
farther open with my tongue.

Her hair was still in that severe bun that made me want
to pull it, so her hair tumbled around her shoulders.

At least today she was in a plaid pencil skirt and
a shapeless cardigan that did nothing for the curves I
remembered.

"Take it off." I pointed to the brown cardigan.

"Excuse me?"

Slater's eyes widened a bit in my direction while Finn

stood behind her, his hands softly moved to her shoulders. "I'll help."

And next on my list.

Finn's murder!

His fingertips grazed her neck as he slowly helped her out of the piece of clothing and then gently laid it on the back of one of our desk chairs.

He winked at me over her head.

I clenched my hands into fists.

He was doing it on purpose. My blood pressure skyrocketed as I tried to regain my focus.

"Kora." Saying her name already had me at half-mast and attempting to tell my brain not to salute.

Shiiiit.

Friendship, friendship, butterflies, puppies. Grandma Jean naked. Wrinkles. Fake teeth in a glass… and there we go! Cured!

"Kora," I tried again, "tell us a little bit about what you need in a relationship to be fulfilled. It sounds like a difficult question, so I'm going to help you out. What is your preference out of the five love languages? Touch? Words of endearment? Acts of service? Gifts? Or time?"

She frowned. "You know, I've never really thought about it but, I would probably put time at the top of that list, even if the time isn't spent doing things together, just being in the same room with someone is comfortable. After that, I would definitely say touch and then words of endearment."

"Good." I scribbled down some notes on her intake. My damn pen was slippery and sliding through my fingertips. It was like I was back in high school, back when she scolded

me for being tardy at least twice a week. God, she'd hated me, and now she was here. Needing something from me.

The teacher from all my fantasies.

My new professor.

I regained my composure. "What did you hate the most about your last relationship?"

Her lower lip trembled, and then she rasped, "Being manipulated. Feeling like I wasn't enough. Hating that I was invisible, and then praying to God that I would be so he wouldn't hurt me... emotionally..." She swallowed. "Physically."

I snapped my pen in half and dropped it out of my hands. "Tell me you're safe from him?"

"As safe as a person can be," she said smoothly, her eyes darting away from mine.

Bullshit.

I took a soothing breath. "So, I think we'll focus our time on rebuilding your self-confidence and helping you understand what you need—and how to ask for it, does that sound okay?"

She gave me a small nod.

I stood and took the wine glass from her hand, handing it to Slater. "We're going to start with words."

"All right." She leaned forward, copying my movements.

"You," I said with conviction, "are absolutely breathtaking."

She sucked in a sharp breath.

"But you're hiding." I moved my hand to her cheek and slid my fingertips up until they touched her silky hair, and then I very slowly pulled the bobby pins from her head and let her long hair fall past her breasts. "There we go."

She gulped. "He said my hair tempted men."

"He was right. He was also jealous." This from Slater as he stood at her side and caressed her arm with the back of his knuckles. "His insecurity was the problem, so he projected it onto you."

She started to shake.

Finn put his hands back down her shoulders. "Breathe."

She inhaled.

"Exhale, slowly, count to five and repeat five more times." His mouth was close to her ear.

I wanted to sucker punch him in the dick.

Both of them actually.

I reached for her hand and squeezed it. "When was the last time you held hands with anyone?"

Her eyes filled with tears. "I don't remember."

"All right." I squeezed. "For the remainder of our session, I'm going to hold your hand, I'm going to caress your leg… and Kora?" My chest tightened. "You. Are. Safe."

She burst into tears.

I wanted to hold her, to kiss each tear away, to tell her that everything was fine, that she had me now—she had us. Instead, I held her hand and then reached for the other.

Her lips trembled as I leaned forward and forgot all about the lust I had for this woman. I looked into her eyes, saw her wounded soul, and just touched her.

Because sometimes all a human being needs…

Is touch from someone else, so they know they aren't alone.

Chapter Eight

"Time is either for you or against you.
It depends on the woman.
Often you need to coax before you kiss."
— Leo Blackwood

Kora

I was a mess.

I wanted to crawl under the nearest desk and hide for the rest of the semester, especially since I was supposed to be the adult, right? At least that's what I felt like my role was supposed to be. Instead, I was having trouble wiping the hot tears from my cheeks while Leo simply held my hand.

For so long, touch had made me either flinch or caused suspicion, because Chadwick had almost always used it as a weapon, and I was so desperate for something—anything—that I gave in every single time.

"Why don't you tell me what you're thinking right now?" Leo asked, his thumb caressing the sensitive inside part of my wrist as another glass of wine just magically appeared in my other hand.

And then fingers whispered across my shoulders followed by a gentle graze of a hand down my thigh, a squeeze, and then nothing.

Their touches never lingered long enough for me to even process something beyond the fact that someone was paying attention to me.

Leo was the only one who held on.

"I, uh…" My voice cracked. "I'm thinking a lot of things."

His lips twitched into a devastating smile that made me sigh out loud as he leaned in and gave me a single nod. "Pick one."

"Okay." Mouth dry, I took a lingering sip of my white wine and then blurted. "It feels nice to know that there's not an ulterior motive. You can't date clients, so you're not giving me wine because you want me drunk but because you want me relaxed. You're touching me for my benefit— not yours. I guess it feels nice to just be selfish for once in my adult—" I almost said adult twice, so he got the idea "—life."

Something flickered in his gaze before he looked away like he needed to regain his composure, but it was so fast I convinced myself I was imaging things because suddenly the smile was back and he was squeezing my hand and then pulling away. "That's what we do. We're happy when you're happy." He stood. "And now it's time to piss you off."

"Huh?" Wait, I wanted more happy time! Bring the happy back!

"You need to learn how to stop letting a man control you. Women are incredibly strong, gifted, talented creatures." He paced in front of me. "Did you know that they're often referred to as the crown of creation in Biblical texts?"

My eyebrows shot up. "Um, no?"

"Ancient civilizations, especially Hebrew ones, revered crowns as a way to describe authority and honor—the highest place given, the highest price paid, the last thing to be created. Think of yourself, Kora, as the great crescendo. Have you been living life on mute, or have you been living it so loud that people have to take notice of your beauty? Your strength? The masterpiece that you are?"

I tried to speak, but I didn't even know what to say. How was a senior in college telling me these things? Why did he make sense? And why was my mouth hanging open like this?

I quickly closed it and then answered. "Sometimes, it's easier to go unnoticed."

"Ah…" Leo winked. "But, the world would be a sad place if it didn't take notice of you."

"Agreed," Finn said behind me. "I think our new client needs an assignment."

"My, my how the tables have turned," Slater said to my left and then nodded to Leo. Was he their leader or something?

"Our time's almost up." Leo crossed his arms. "Which means homework for the professor." His face lit up like it amused him, I wasn't sure if I wanted to strangle him or kiss him for the breakthrough.

Then again, I was a client.

No kissing, right?

No anything.

It was best that way.

I couldn't imagine a girl not getting attached when an attractive guy with low slung jeans and an eight-pack told her she was the crown of creation.

I mean, hello? Tinder was full of dick pics.

So it made sense.

"Lay it on me." I smiled.

Leo licked his lips, his eyes darting to my mouth briefly before he looked away and said, "No more buns and you have to wear a color, any color, it can be fire engine red for all I care, but something that makes you happy, brings attention, and most importantly, wear something *he* would fucking hate."

I laughed at that.

The rest of the guys chuckled with me.

Man, it felt good to laugh about that idiot.

"All right." I stood. "I'll try."

"Don't try, do." Leo winked. "Wouldn't wanna give you an F on your first assignment, not to our new star student."

"Cute." I rolled my eyes. "I see what you did there."

He shrugged a shoulder. "It's only fair."

"True." I stared at him harder, wondering when the boy from high school had grown into this wise man with all the muscles and the ability to tilt my world on its axis all through a smug grin and an easy wink.

"So…" Finn coughed. "Use the Wingmen portal to set up your next session. We typically do three to six for first-timers, depending on their needs. And we'll send you an appointment reminder when the time gets closer."

I let out a long exhale. "Great. Thanks."

Slater opened the door to the main living room and then took the glass from my hand with an easy smile. "You did well."

"Thanks for the help." I was practically floating.

"It's what we do," Leo said from behind him, his gaze locking onto mine with an intensity that made my entire body heat with longing.

No. Bad.

Student. Student.

Well, I guess now I was the student, and he was the teacher?

Ugh.

Either way. Bad. All bad.

But it would be good.

"She okay?" Finn asked out loud while I mentally warred with my own conscience.

"YUP!" I nearly yelled. "Sorry, thoughts, lots of… um, thoughts."

Leo bit down on his lower lip like he knew exactly where my thoughts were going, and his eyes gave me the inclination that he wanted to meet me there.

Several. Times.

"Okay then!" I nearly tripped over my own bag in my rush to leave and then saw a woman in tears standing outside their door. It was a reality check that I desperately needed. I was in a dorm room for God's sake! A dorm room! And this was their job.

I straightened my spine a bit and walked around the upset girl so the guys could take care of her.

My heart felt like it lost a bit of its happy. Why did that bother me?

"Carli, everything okay?" Slater put his hand on her shoulder.

"C-can we have an emergency session?"

"Of course," he said smoothly as he wrapped an arm around her and led her into the room.

The door shut.

And that was it.

I almost laughed.

I was really reading into this.

It was their *job* to make me feel good, to make my heart flutter, to make me feel alive.

And they were damn good at it.

Too good.

Because for the first time in years, I had a smile on my face and wanted nothing more than to wear something that wasn't black.

Something that showed off my curves.

The hell with it, I was going shopping.

And I was buying heels.

Chapter Nine

"Never take your sexual frustrations out on your pillow.
First off, gross.
Second, that's why she probably thinks of you as a eunuch.
Third, your pillow is where you put your other head, dipshit."
— *Leo Blackwood.*

Leo

I was a sexually frustrated, friend-zoned mess.

And I hated everyone.

Most of all, Finn and Slater. Not really for doing anything other than touching her, pouring her more wine, getting a few smiles—all that I could deal with. I mean, I'd just beat the shit out of them later. But the fact that she seemed to respond to them just as much as me? Not cool.

But the giant cherry on top of all of this chaos?

She *knew* I couldn't do shit about the way I felt.

She'd said as much.

Out loud.

To my face.

And then smiled such a gorgeous freeing smile that I

felt like the worst sort of bastard for even wanting to break the rules of the Wingmen contract.

I'd never been tempted to quit.

But she made me want to just so I could do something stupid like throw her up against a sturdy wall, spread those legs wide and have my way with her.

It wasn't just the physical, though. It was her emotional response, the way that she seemed so starved for words and touch that I wanted to be the lucky bastard giving them to her.

And not for a price.

But because I wanted to give it.

Hell.

I drummed my fingertips against my desk, too confused to do anything but stare at my stupid computer screen and magically pray for something to appear like a scalding email from my favorite prof.

Nothing.

The guys had gone to grab tacos and the hum of the computer plus the soft sounds of Drake, yeah right, in the background made me want to commit a crime.

I clicked out of my email and into the Wingmen app.

"This isn't stalking, it's business." And I was officially talking to myself.

I scanned her social media info and quickly followed her on Instagram and Facebook and kept scrolling.

Her number.

Right there.

Her cell.

It would be easy to take advantage.

Easy to just send a *"hang in there"* text.

Friends did that all the time, right?

I vaguely remembered the part where I signed a contract saying I wouldn't use any client information for anything personal, but this wasn't personal, right? It was just a Wingmen coach calling up his client to say "s'up?"

Wow. Had I really fallen that low?

Before the angel on my shoulder could tell me no, I programmed her number into my phone high fived the devil on the other side and shot off a quick text.

> Me: This is your official check-in. Make sure you hydrate this evening and remember your homework.

There that sounded professional, right?

She texted right back.

> Kora: Is this Finn?

I imagined running him over with my car.

> Me: No.

> Kora: Slater?

And now Slater was going to get suffocated with a pillow.

> Me: No.

And nothing.

Seriously?

I gaped at my screen until finally, the little dots appeared, and she responded.

> Kora: Leo then?

Me: Took you long enough.

That… didn't sound professional, but I was annoyed as hell! Why would they be her first picks? I mean Finn? He still cried during Titanic! He said it was because he had allergies, but we all knew he was full of shit!

Kora: Do you talk to all your clients that way?

Friend. Friend. Friend. Be the friend. Don't let her provoke you. I took a much-needed deep breath and responded.

Me: I like to think of it as tough love. Just remember to let us know if you need anything and know that it's normal to feel a bit drained afterward.

Kora: Drained how?

Me: Emotionally. Physically.

Kora: Interesting. I actually feel… revived a bit.

No idea why, but the word "revive" had my dick twitching in a very reviving way, if you get my meaning. *FRIEND, you loser, we're her friend!*

Me: How so?

Kora: I don't know. I just feel like I've taken a nice hot bath, you know, with the expensive bath bombs.

Me: The only kind to use, Lush all the way.

Kora: Lol, I should say I'm surprised you know, then again, it's kind of your job, right? Anyways, yes, lush bath bomb experience, that's what it felt like, so thank you.

I ground my teeth.

> Me: It's not just my job...
>
> Kora: Don't.
>
> Me: Don't what?
>
> Kora: Hit on me. Not now.

Deflated, I stared at the phone in my hand and finally responded.

> Me: It's against the rules. I just want you to know, I would do this for any friend, not just because you need it, which you do, but because you deserve all the good things—all the Lush bath bombs.
>
> Kora: What makes you think I deserve anything good?
>
> Me: What makes you think you don't?

She didn't respond for a while and then finally ended our conversation.

> Kora: Headed to bed. Thanks again.

So that was it. My game sucked even via text messages, which was where ugly dudes usually took the cake: *I'm so funny, I'm so caring, but don't be pissed when I have a unibrow, cool?*

I exhaled a frustrated breath and looked back at my computer screen.

Her address.

With a smile, I suddenly knew what I was going to do.

"Get ready, Kora, I don't give up easily."

And there I went talking to myself again as I clicked open a new website and typed in my search.

Chapter Ten

*"Gifts aren't meant to be used as a tool of manipulation but as
a way to make the object of your affection feel important.
If you're keeping score, you're going to die alone."*
— *Leo Blackwood*

Kora

I woke up Wednesday feeling like I could conquer the
world—and then I looked at my phone.

More missed calls from Chadwick.

And a text with a question mark.

I deleted the text, ignored the calls, and decided I would
deal with him later. Of course, I wanted him to finally sign
the paperwork, but it felt like it was just another excuse for
him to talk to me about getting back together.

My stomach rolled.

The idea of going to the wedding with him, whether
driving in a car or on an airplane, made me want to pack
my own parachute and mace.

I shuddered and went into the kitchen to make some
coffee when I heard a knock on my apartment door.

I checked the clock on the microwave. It was nine in the morning, the mail wouldn't be there yet, and I wasn't expecting anyone.

A cold chill ran down my spine.

Did he have my address?

It wasn't public, but he was rich. He could get it if he really wanted to.

I looked out the peephole first, saw nothing, waited a few minutes, then opened the door a crack.

Nothing down the hall.

I took a step out and bumped something with my foot.

A package?

Huh.

I smiled down at it. Dumb, but I hadn't gotten a package or present from anyone in who knew how long? My parents weren't big on birthdays or holidays and often traveled abroad for Christmas.

I gave the box a little shake and brought it into my apartment then attacked it with a knife.

It smelled amazing.

What was it?

Purple tissue paper was taped together with a note on the inside.

"Remember your assignments."

—XOXO Leo

My smile actually hurt my face as I tugged open the tissue paper and saw at least two hundred dollars' worth of Lush bath bombs.

And then tears stung the back of my eyes as I realized

it was the first gift I'd been given… that didn't have strings attached.

I quickly pulled out my cell and sent Leo a text.

> Me: Thank you for the bath bombs. I can't wait to come home tonight.
>
> Leo: THAT right there, is music to my ears. Home should be your sanctuary. Enjoy, Kora.

I shivered at his mention of my name, and the guy wasn't even saying it. I just imagined the caress of his mouth as he murmured it.

Damn it.

Talk about inappropriate thoughts about a student. I could have some very, very inappropriate ones about him.

At least the client contract protected us on both sides— him from continuing to blatantly hit on me, and me from falling for his ridiculous charm.

And yet, when I went to my room to get ready and stood in front of my closet, it was Leo I thought about.

When I went to my lingerie drawer and bypassed my Spanx in favor of a lacy black pair of boy shorts, when I went to the bathroom and added a bright pink lip gloss and a bit of mascara, when I put on a pair of tall heels, when I put on my leather pencil skirt and tucked my pale blouse in.

I imagined him the entire drive to school.

And smiled as I sent him a quick text that said, "Hope I get an A."

Chapter Eleven

"Nothing better than a woman
who knows her way around a nice, crisp red apple.
See also: Bite me next."
— Leo Blackwood

Leo

High School Senior Year

"**Y**ou're late, Blackwood." Mrs. Robinson didn't even turn away from the smart board as I slumped into my desk and flashed a smile toward her perfect ass.

Was it wrong to stare? Yes.

Could I help myself? I growled. That would be a hell no.

"Sorry." I finally got the word out. "I'll try harder next time, Mrs. R."

"Try any harder and brain cells will start dying," she teased, looking at me over her shoulder playfully.

I barked out a laugh. "Easy, my ego may die along with them."

The room erupted into laughs from the guys, sighs from the girls.

"Hardly likely." She smiled and then grabbed the US History book. "All right, open to page sixty-nine."

My entire body tightened with awareness. The class chuckled. I was too busy locking eyes with my teacher.

Hers were narrowed on me.

But they stayed there for a solid three seconds before she cleared her throat and looked away.

Anyone watching would think it was a death stare.

They wouldn't notice the erratic pulse at the base of her neck or the way she shifted on her feet as if she was trying to clench her thighs.

But I noticed everything about her.

Always would.

She was the only teacher who gave me shit.

Who forced me to work hard when the rest passed me because I was the quarterback.

Sometimes I wondered if she was the only one who saw me at all.

Class went by in a blur. I grabbed my backpack and started to put my books away.

"Blackwood." She barked out my name. "Stay for a minute."

"Leo's in trouble again..." Eustice teased jogging by me toward the gym, where we had practice in a half hour.

Students shuffled out, and then it was just her and me.

I strutted over to her desk and crossed my arms. "Finally admitting that you like me, Mrs. R?"

"Mrs." *She repeated the word with heavy emphasis.* "Means I'm taken, and even if I wasn't... Prison."

"I'm eighteen."

She scowled. "Leo, you can't keep coming to class late."

"I have straight A's," *I pointed out.*

"That's not the point." *She stood, and it felt like she was towering over me when the exact opposite was true.* "People follow you. Whether you like it or not you're a leader to the underclassmen, can you at least try to be a good example, so we don't have a million seniors like you next year?"

I smiled at that. "You sound genuinely worried I'm gonna haunt the place."

Her cheeks went pink. "I'm serious."

"And I'm not?" *I leaned forward.* "You have really pretty eyes, you know."

"Leo." *Her tone was scathing.* "What works on your other female teachers won't work on me."

"I know."

She rolled her eyes.

"Because I don't compliment my other teachers. And before you say anything, I think Mrs. Turner has wonderful hair despite the lazy eye."

She pressed her lips tighter like she was trying not to smile.

"And that brief issue with gout." *I leaned closer.* "It's okay to laugh."

She sighed and looked away. "Promise me you'll try."

"I'll do better." *I reached out and grabbed one of her pens, then started flipping it between my fingers.* "I'll do it. But only because you asked nicely and because you have a solid *point—I would feel horrible if you cried yourself to sleep next year because every male student reminded you of me."*

She coughed out a laugh. "You keep telling yourself that."

"Don't have to." I shrugged. "I see it in your eyes."

"Leo." Her nostrils flared.

"Our secret." I handed her back her pen. She took it, and our fingers brushed longer than necessary. And hers? Were trembling. "And Mrs. Robinson?"

"Yes." Her voice cracked.

"Even if you don't miss me, know that I'll miss you. A lot." I flashed her a genuine smile and gave her my back.

I jolted awake from the memory, nightmare, dream, I wasn't even sure what it was other than my brain reminding me that I'd had it bad for my teacher for over four years.

Damn it.

A few minutes later, I got a text and felt my body grow in all the wrong and inappropriate places as Kora said she hoped she would get an A.

Fuck. Me.

"Bro." Slater covered his eyes. "If you're watching porn—"

"I'm not watching porn, you ass! I just woke up!"

"Sure, sure." He laughed and threw a pillow at me. "Don't you have class in an hour?"

"Shit." I wiped my face with my hands, grabbed my shit, and made my way out the door just in time for Slater to yell.

"Make it cold!"

I flipped him off and indeed took a frigid shower, all the

while wondering how the hell I would survive if she actually did try today.

It bothered me the entire way to get coffee.

And then, as I walked down the hall and took a deep breath in front of the classroom door.

It would be fine; she was just a woman.

A very, very attractive woman.

I was fine.

Right?

Ridiculous.

I walked into the room and quickly took my seat. Huh, she wasn't there. I mean, there was a woman up front, but her back was to us.

Just as she turned, I took a swig of coffee.

And started choking.

The girl sitting behind me began slapping my back so hard I almost herniated, all the while Kora smiled up at me, amusement dancing in her eyes. "You gonna make it, Blackwood?"

I've never understood the term swallowing your own tongue. How is that physically possible?

And yet.

My tongue felt swollen, I couldn't breathe well, and I wondered if this was the moment people were talking about, when your tongue had nowhere else to go except out your mouth like a dog or to the back of your throat.

"Er—" I rasped. "Yes, ma'am, yes."

Smooth.

"Good." Her leather pencil skirt was tight against her thighs. As she moved around the room, her clothes hugged every curve, I was a cat, she was a scrumptious mouse I wanted to pounce on and—

Oh shit, she was asking people to read.

I shoved all thoughts of her perfection away even though it was difficult, especially when I couldn't stop fixating on the loose braid that hung past her shoulder. A few hairs fell out, and she kept tucking them back until finally putting a pencil behind her ear, just fucking flaming every schoolboy fantasy to life yet again.

I gripped my desk with both hands, fingertips going completely white as she finally dismissed class.

A few idiots stayed back to ask her a question.

One dipshit made her laugh.

Ruining his life later.

And there I sat.

Finally, her almond-shaped blue eyes lifted to mine. "Blackwood."

Down boy. "Mrs. R."

She grinned wide. "Why does it feel like the roles are reversed?"

I stood and grabbed my bag then slowly made my way down the stairs until I was right in front of her, measuring her short breaths and the nervous way she licked those pink lips. "I like a good role reversal."

"I bet."

I laughed and pulled the pencil from her ear, letting the escaped pieces of hair kiss her cheek. Never been jealous of hair but there's a first time for everything.

I put a hand on her shoulder and very gently leaned in and whispered. "A-minus."

"What?" She jerked back. "Are you sure you don't mean A-plus?"

"Oh, she wants extra credit now?" I teased.

Her scowl was adorable. "I did good."

"Good isn't great though, is it?"

She stomped her foot.

Holy shit, I was keeping this woman forever. She just didn't know it yet.

"An A-minus is bullshit." She said in a gravelly voice I was instantly responding to.

"Well, the extra credit shouldn't take too long anyway, but it's kind of… daring." I shrugged. "And no offense… but…" I didn't finish my sentence, and once again, I could tell she was wondering if she could stab me in the dick with her pencil and get away with claiming self-defense.

"Fine." She crossed her arms. "What is it?"

My eyebrows shot up. "Something a good girl wouldn't do, that's for sure."

"What does that have to do with Wingmen?" she asked.

"Confidence is everything. You gotta know how to fake it, especially in the presence of assholes."

"Like you?"

I grinned. "Easy, I meant like your ex. Why, do I look like an emotional terrorist?"

She deflated a bit. I hated it. "What's my extra credit?"

I looked over my shoulder to make sure the door was closed, then stepped toward it, pulled the blinds down, and turned the lock.

Her eyes widened.

"Relax." I made my way back to her. "I'm not going to seduce you. Can't, remember? It's in my contract."

"I know that."

Sure she did.

"Your next class will be here in less than fifteen minutes. So you have exactly—" I checked my Rolex "—eleven minutes to get this done."

"Get what done?"

"Panties." I held out my hand. "Now."

"Excuse me!" Yeah, I was definitely getting murdered today. "I'm not giving you my underwear, you perv!"

"Chill, I'm not keeping them." I rolled my eyes. "Take them off, and I'll give them back to you."

"But I have one more class."

"Yup."

"And I have to walk around."

"Yup."

She glared. "Is that all you're going to say? And if you say yup, I'm shoving a pencil into your aorta."

"That's alarmingly graphic," I muttered. "And you now have ten minutes."

She looked around the room, probably realizing what I already knew, there was no place to really hide, her desk was too short, and we were in an auditorium.

"Nine minutes," I said in a bored voice.

"I hate you," she muttered.

"Most paying customers do at first," I said truthfully. "You're running low on time... Mrs. R."

With one more scowl my way, she started hiking up her leather skirt and then paused at her thighs. "Turn around."

"No." I shrugged. "Hurry up."

"So. Wrong," she said to herself as she finally got her skirt high enough right at her hips, and then her perfect fingers were tugging down a lacy pair of black boy shorts.

It was over too fast.

Her skirt was back down.

Her panties were in her hand. "Happy?"

I sauntered over to her and wrapped an arm around her waist, then very slowly slid my hand down her back and cupped her ass. "Just checking your work."

Her gaze was heavy, and it was on my mouth. "A-plus?"

"Plus, plus," I leaned down, knowing it was wrong, knowing it was against policy, but she met me halfway, her hands gripping my biceps, nails digging into my skin.

And then a knock sounded at the door.

We broke apart.

I cursed and jabbed a finger at her. "Put them in your purse, you can put them back on after class is done, but I think you might enjoy the freedom of having them off all day."

"I doubt it." Her smile was forced.

"I'm a professional, remember?" It was like I was reminding both of us.

Her nod was short, curt.

And I was back at square one as I unlocked the door and jerked it open only to come face to face with her son of a bitch ex-husband and his fucking black glasses.

Chapter Twelve

"Nothing feels better than skin on skin—
unless you're wearing leather and then I want both.
I'm a greedy SOB, what can I say?"
— Leo Blackwood

Kora

I couldn't see his face, but I felt him, in a way that made my stomach roll. Please let Leo stay.

"You again? Is this a joke?" Chadwick raised his voice then looked around Leo. "You weren't answering my calls."

"I know." I lifted my chin. "I've been busy."

"With this guy?"

Leo stood up against Chadwick, chest to chest. It was almost amusing how much bigger Leo was. Even though he was a college student, he was all man in that moment.

Mine.

No.

"No." I crossed my arms. "With my job, and now my next class will be here soon. Could you please just go?"

"Not until you tell me why you were alone with him!"

Chadwick shoved at Leo, but Leo didn't move. Instead, he slowly turned and shared a look with me.

"I'm her new TA. We locked the door because we were discussing something private about one of the students cheating on the last exam, and with social media, you never know what people might do or say or take the wrong way." He looked back at Chadwick. "Am I right?"

Chadwick's eyes narrowed. "A coincidence then?"

"It's a small world." Leo patted Chadwick on the shoulder. "Looks like her next class is starting to trickle in." Sure enough, students bypassed the men blocking the door as I stood there in stunned disbelief. "You should make an appointment. Her office hours are taped to the door."

"Are you shitting me right now?" Chadwick muttered.

"Or if you want," Leo flashed him an easy grin. "I can pull up her calendar and pencil you in. How does next week Monday sound? Five p.m.?"

"What the hell," he said, mainly to himself. "I guess, sure, I mean…" He eyed me again. "Is that the soonest we can talk?"

"Sorry." I shrugged helplessly. "I've had to take on a lot of classes."

I hoped to God he got the jab, felt it in between his ribs.

I'd taken nothing from him yet, and still, he wasn't signing the papers.

And now I had to work twice as hard to make a living.

More students bypassed him.

"Fine, fine." He shot Leo a look. "Have her text a reminder to me so my secretary can put it on my calendar, all right?"

"Of course. It's what a good TA does." Leo beamed.

And then escorted the nightmare from my classroom, shutting the door quietly behind him.

I would have cheered had I not had ninety humans staring at me expectantly.

And an hour later, when class was done, I actually did do a little cheer because Leo had texted me.

> Leo: Sent a note to security. They'll be there to escort your ex from the building on Monday. I'll be conveniently taking a test next door to your office. Oh, and I accidentally tripped him in the parking lot. Also, I like you better without him clouding your sunlight. XoXo, Leo

I stared from the phone to my purse where my underwear was waiting, and with confidence I hadn't felt in years, I grabbed my stuff and strutted out of the classroom only to nearly run directly into Slater and Finn in the hall.

"Guys?" Oh no, would people know I was a client? Could I get in trouble?

"Hey there, Professor Robinson," Slater said a bit too loudly for my taste. He held out a cup of coffee and whispered. "It's not coffee."

I took it, realizing too late my hands were trembling from seeing him again, the evil ex from hell. "Huh?"

"Leo said you could use some liquid courage and since you're not driving home for a few hours... why not?" Finn added.

"You know..." Slater grinned, instantly making me feel at ease. "We had a cancelation tonight."

I took a sip. Wine. It was wine. I almost giggled. "How sad for you."

"I know, right?" Finn agreed, leaning his large body closer, the faint smell of cologne filled the space between us. The effect was more calming than anything. "If you want us to add you in, we heard you did a good job with your homework, and Leo's anxious to get you to the next level."

"Next level being what?" I asked, taking another small sip from the paper coffee cup and finally calming down enough to be decent.

"Caterpillar…" Finn held out one hand, "Butterfly…" He pointed at me. "But we still have some inside work to do. You know, intense heart therapy. Let us know, or if you want Leo to shit himself, just show up. Eight o'clock."

"That's a nice mental picture." I laughed.

Finn shrugged. "Think about it beautiful."

I gulped when he put his hand on my shoulder, gently caressing me with two fingertips before walking off with Slater.

Seriously? Did they train for that sort of thing?

Why was my shoulder still buzzing with awareness when I didn't even like him?

They left me staring after them. Girls whispered and took pictures as they moved through the large hall.

They did a good job of ignoring all the attention even when it was negative attention from jealous guys.

Eight tonight.

Ridiculous. I mean, I had things to do!

Stuart, for one, could starve, I always fed him right at seven. And cats lived and died by their schedules! Right?

Plus, I had papers to read and grade!

And I was going to watch The Voice because I'd missed last week's episode, and…

Oh God, was that my life?

The reason I wasn't taking them up on another appointment?

If last night worked wonders, what would tonight do?

Just thinking about it gave me goosebumps.

Plus, then I could thank Leo. I did owe him.

But I mean, it would be in a totally platonic way.

As I ripped his T-shirt with my teeth and tugged his jeans down.

Platonic.

Someone slap me.

"Professor Robinson, are you okay?" A timid freshman named Cali asked me, the poor thing still had braces and was so quiet during class I could barely understand her.

"Yes, I'm sorry, I was just thinking about something."

Her grin brightened as she hugged her books to her chest. "Must have been something awesome like dessert."

"Yes." I nodded. "It was just like… dessert."

"Well, have a bite for me!" She skipped off, and I was left with nothing but visions of biting Leo.

And Leo…

Biting me right back.

Chapter Thirteen

"If you're not thinking of me naked at least three times a day—I'm doing life wrong."
— *Leo Blackwood*

Leo

Lacy boy shorts, who knew?

I tapped my pen against my denim-clad thigh and tried to focus on my computer screen, on the very boring paper I had to write for my human ethics class.

I let out a snort. Ironic that I was writing a paper on ethics while thinking about my professor naked.

But damn, she'd actually done it.

Had stepped out of those lacy things and stared me down while doing it.

Shit, if I kept thinking about it, I was going to have to take care of a very serious problem, and we had rules about that sort of thing when we had clients, Wingmen wanted us to be sexually charged and focused, something about the energy in the room.

Well, Maranda was definitely going to feel my sexual

frustration in about five minutes. I was hard as nails, and I'd written two paragraphs before daydreaming about Kora biting into an apple and sitting on her desk, I'd spread her thighs and...

"Knock, knock," Finn's voice sounded before he shoved the door open.

I frowned and pointed my pen in his direction. "I don't like that smile."

He was wearing his usual uniform, jeans and a black T-shirt that showed off a bit of chest tattoo that usually drove the females wild.

"Well, that's offensive." He grinned harder. "Don't you think that's offensive, Slater?"

"Gotta be honest bro, I'm wounded on your behalf." Slater put a hand against his chest and shook his head. "Besides, you have a sexy smile."

"Dude." Finn held out his fist, "That came from the heart, thank you for this moment."

"Helllll!" I spun around in my chair. "Why are you dipshits being like this? Why? You're both a pain in my ass, and you're wearing your plotting faces."

"What?" Slater looked behind him. "This face? This one right here."

"That one." I crossed my arms.

"This is the only face I have though." Slater shot a wink in my direction. "Plus, the ladies love it, some men too."

"Do you bro," Finn said.

They high fived.

I let out a groan and stood. "Whatever, I'm not gonna push it. We need to set up for Maranda."

"Canceled." Finn whistled. "She canceled a few hours ago. I figured you were busy with your homework." He craned his neck to stare at my computer. "Wow, two hours, and you have two paragraphs. You have a mild stroke in between sentences, or are the words just too big this time?"

I flipped him off. "I'm distracted."

"By global warming?" Slater asked. "The upcoming election?"

"World hunger." Finn snapped his fingers. "Remember, our Leo has a big heart."

"What the hell is with you guys today?" I threw my pen then searched for another one only to come up empty. "Can't a guy just be distracted?"

Finn laughed. "Bro, if you were any more sexually frustrated, I would feel sorry for you."

"Wait," I growled. "Why don't you feel sorry for me now?"

"It's amusing." Slater grabbed a football and sat on my bed. "Amusing as hell, actually."

"One day—" I jabbed my finger at him, my back to the open door. "—I pray for the day you're as sexually frustrated as I am, so fucking hard over a piece of fruit that—"

"Knock, knock." A familiar feminine voice broke in. "Sorry, I just figured I should interrupt before that got any weirder."

I groaned into my hands.

"To be fair…" Slater looked around my body at Kora. "Could it get weirder?"

"Asking for a friend," Finn added in.

"Meh, depends on the fruit."

I could smell her as she waltzed past me and sat in my desk chair. Her perfume did funny things to my heart and my dick, no judgment, I was sexually frustrated all right?

"Woman has a point," Slater agreed, the bastard. "So, I guess the only question we have—"

"You know, other than the one where we ask where this odd fascination began," Finn offered helpfully.

"Yes, other than that minor detail." Slater waved him off. "What's the fruit in question?"

"Can't be a banana." Finn tapped his chin. "Too close to his own equipment."

"Compare my dick to a banana again and I'm selling you on the black market." I clenched my teeth.

"He'd go for millions!" Slater burst out laughing. "Okay, so no bananas… This is a conundrum."

"We didn't have an appointment today." I ignored them and changed the subject. Kora hadn't changed, meaning her curves were in full view as she sat with her legs crossed looking so prim and proper I wanted to dirty her up.

All in all, I was dying a slow, painful death of want.

And she had no idea.

Because she trusted me.

Because I was her coach now.

Her friend.

Yeah, I was seconds from jumping out the window and putting myself out of my misery.

"Oh, I know." She beamed. "The guys invited me because I did so good on my homework and extra credit." That was followed by a wink I felt everywhere.

"Apple." Finn guessed loudly. "You bought a shit ton of apples last week."

I shot him a death glare.

"What?" He shrugged. "An apple a day keeps the doctor away."

"That's what I always say." Slater nodded seriously. "Getting sick's no joke, gotta take care of you, ya know?"

"Bro, you speak to my soul." Finn teased.

Had they always been this annoying?

"How nice of Leo to share with me, then," Kora said softly, her eyes sparkling in my direction. I wanted to get lost in those eyes. I'd always dreamed of the day when she would look at me like I was a man, grown up, no longer her student.

Right now, she was looking at me like that.

Two seconds of torture later and her teasing smile was directed at the guys, the look she had given me, gone.

"He's a giver, Leo." Slater stood. "All right, should we get started with round two?"

"Round two, lesson two," Finn joined in. "I think this is the perfect time, and Kora, I think you're ready."

I was getting ready to pull my shirt off. Lesson two often involved more touching, but we let her explore, build her confidence in a way that she knew how to ask for what she wanted when she was with her person.

Skin on skin was necessary, especially with her. She was gun shy for good reason.

Just thinking about her ex showing up today had me ready to rip the room to shreds.

Once an asshole, always an asshole.

"Leo." Finn shot me a look I couldn't decipher. "I'm going to have Slater take this one. You'll sit out and watch."

I clenched my fists. "I'm sorry, what?"

"You," Finn spoke slowly. "Sit. And she'll touch Slater and me while you instruct her what to do."

Could he be any more condescending?

I knew why I was sitting out.

I wasn't stupid.

He didn't want her touching me because I was so strung up. It would probably be impossible to hide how aroused I was.

Kora took a deep breath.

I smiled so she would feel at ease when really all I wanted to do was leap across the room and pull her into my arms, beg her to let me prove to her that this wasn't just infatuation.

This could be something more.

More than just helping her get over the asshole and live her life.

I hated that I was helping to teach her how to come out of her shell and loathed the idea that some other guy would be the one to appreciate it when nobody deserved her.

Not even me.

Chapter Fourteen

"Always make them want more… if you fail, you gave way
too much of the milk to the cow, you know?"
— Leo Blackwood

Kora

The amount of testosterone in that room was nearly overwhelming. I was having a hard time not staring as Slater and Finn both took off their shirts.

Leo sat on the bed across from me, his stare emotionless, but his hands clenched into tight fists like he was ready to throw punches at any minute.

"All right," Leo said smoothly. "For this lesson, we're going to try to make touching good, not bad. No flinching, no shying away, and most importantly, we want you to feel free to…" His voice cracked. "Explore."

Was it my imagination, or did a muscle jump in his jaw?

Was he clenching his teeth?

I frowned at him only to have him give me an answering smile in return.

Cleary, I was imagining things, maybe because I wanted to. Because I wanted to be touching him—freely.

I about died when I walked in on his conversation. I knew the guys were just giving him crap, but part of me wondered if it was true—not the apples, but maybe because he was giving them to me?

I was reaching.

He made me want to.

"Kora?" The way Leo said my name was like a whisper of a kiss across my lips. "Do you understand?"

"Yes." I gulped. "I'm not sure how good I'm going to be at this."

"People who are used to hiding are typically horrible at it, so don't feel bad. Again, we're here to help you not to make you feel bad, so if you need to stop, you stop, you call all the shots." His eyes locked with mine. "Understand?"

"Yes."

"But just in case," Slater piped up, "your safe word is apple."

I cracked a smile as Leo rolled his eyes.

"Let's begin," Leo snapped. "Slater's going to stand in front of you. he's going to lean in and touch your face, then he's going to caress down your arms, nothing serious."

Slater's hands instantly cupped my cheeks, I wondered in that moment why I wasn't attracted to him, he was beautiful to look at, with bright green eyes, an easy smile, and a muscular chest.

His lips almost looked swollen, and I wondered if he was the type to use his mouth as a weapon, sucking and licking until the woman screamed his name.

Those same soft hands moved down my neck. A place I would normally shy away from being touched; it felt too vulnerable.

My body started to shake a bit as his hands moved to my shoulders and then down.

He did this at least a dozen times, but with each time I got more and more relaxed until finally, I enjoyed the feel of his hands and the freedom of being able to stop him at any time.

"Now," Leo's voice sounded hoarse. His green eyes stayed focused on me. "It's your turn."

"My turn?" I repeated.

"Finn." He ignored me while Slater left, and Finn stood in front of me, he was taller than Slater, leaner with a runner's body. And maybe I was being ridiculous, but I'd always wondered what a really sculpted six-pack looked like in person.

My ex had been thin and was a cycling enthusiast. While his calves were giant, the rest of his body had always felt small. It was even a point of insecurity for me.

"Go ahead," Finn whispered his smile was easy going, nothing sexual about it. "Good touch only."

"What does that mean? I can't pinch you?"

Leo barked out a laugh. "That's adorable, Kora. No, what Finn means is please refrain from grabbing his cock."

My eyes widened. "People do that?"

"If they like nice things they do," Finn joked.

"Oh God, not this again." Slater sighed. "Finn, remember your job doesn't involve using your mouth."

Finn grinned down at me. "Pity."

"Finn." Leo's voice had a warning edge to it.

"Sorry." He looked anything but sorry. "Go ahead Kora, knock yourself out."

"Ummm, okay," I wasn't sure where to touch first, how to touch. It felt stupid, and then I realized I didn't even know what he would like.

I suddenly felt like I was back in high school, trying not to make a fool out of myself in front of the captain of the soccer team.

"Kora," Leo's voice was a bit closer, "Are you okay?"

"Yeah," I rasped. "I just don't know what I'm doing."

"I'll help," He got up and stood next to me. "Do I have your permission to help?"

I gave him a jerky nod.

He moved behind me and then very gently grabbed each of my wrists, lifting my hands toward Finn.

I felt Leo's lips on my ear as he whispered. "Men don't care where you touch as long as it's you touching. You can go soft," He ran my hand down Finn's flat stomach and then turned my hand over, so my knuckles grazed on the way up to his chest. "Or you can go hard," He spread my palm wide and pressed it down on Finn's shoulder. My fingers magically dug into muscle while Finn's eyes did this sexy lazy look that had me thinking of hands gripping sheets, screams of pleasure, and dirty talk.

"That's it," Leo encouraged. "See, even though I'm the one helping you, he can't help but physically respond because it feels good, and guys are turned on by sight first, then touch, meaning when you do both at the same time, you overwhelm the senses."

"Wow." I started exploring more freely, even though Leo was still guiding me.

"Good girl," he whispered in my ear, and this time his teeth grazed my sensitive skin; that simple touch went all the way down my toes as my body buzzed with awareness.

Finn closed his eyes while I slowly ran my hands back down his stomach, and that was when it clicked. All three of them were helping me. Leo was as much a participant as Finn and Slater.

They were getting paid for this.

I was benefitting.

"How much time do we have left?" I asked, feeling slightly drugged off the heady feeling of control.

Leo moved away from me. "About five minutes, why?"

"Last time you said I could earn extra credit," I dropped my hands and turned in my chair as Leo towered over me, his face unreadable. "So, what's my extra credit now?"

His eyes narrowed. "You mean, what would we do next if we had more time? Or what would we have you do?"

I nodded. "Professors want to be star students too."

He barked out a laugh. "Yeah, okay, normally we would do a little holding where you don't flinch and you let the guy hold you from behind, it's to make you feel safe, less triggered so that when it happens in real life you enjoy it."

"Do it."

He exhaled roughly, "Yeah okay, Finn—"

"Not Finn, you."

Leo's eyes flashed. "I'm not sure that's the best id—"

"Please?"

His jaw flexed.

Finn cleared his throat. "Actually, we have a study group in a few minutes. Come on Slater, let's let Leo finish up."

Leo's surprised look told me everything and nothing all at once.

They were leaving the apple-obsessed, sexually frustrated one with me?

Was that the best idea?

"Yup." Slater put his shirt back on, and within minutes they were gone, the door closed.

I was alone with my student.

And I didn't realize until that moment how desperately I'd wanted that.

We had been alone in the classroom, but this was different.

More personal.

More sexual.

In fact, I was choking from the sexual tension in the air. I could almost reach out and touch it.

Leo circled me. "Are you ready, Kora?"

I shivered. "Yes."

"Are you sure?"

"No," I answered honestly. "Just do it already."

Without warning, he spun me around and tilted my chin toward him. "Those exact words are what we're trying to avoid, it's why you're here. Things should never be rushed in order to get them over with. The only time I make an exception is when you can't stop yourself." His thumb rubbed my lower lip. "When you're so taken over by pure need that you have no choice but to rip clothes, slam into

walls, cause a fucking mess over the fact that you can't keep your hands off each other."

My lips parted as my heart slammed against my chest. He was hypnotizing me with his words.

Tempting me beyond reason.

He lowered his head and then spun me around again, so my ass was pressed against him.

He. Was. Huge.

And wedged quite literally exactly where my body needed him.

I let out a little moan.

"Fuck," He rested his head against mine, and then his mouth was on my neck, nipping, tasting. "I can't draw the line with you... I'm sorry."

I leaned back against his length and whispered. "Who said I liked lines anyway?"

His arms tightened around me. "You're a client."

"Yeah."

"There are about a million reasons why this is a horrible idea."

"I know."

"And one reason that matters more than all of them," He loosened his arms and then moved his hands to my hips gripping me there, holding me, I imagined him bending me over his desk as chills erupted across my skin. Warm lips tickled my ear as he spoke. "I. Want. You."

I didn't have time to think as he turned me around and, as promised, pressed me against the wall and slammed his mouth over mine.

I held onto his shoulder with one hand and dug my

other hand into his hair, tugging it hard, pulling him into me as he groaned into my mouth.

His hands slid down my skirt then effortlessly hiked it up until he slid a hand up my thigh.

"Damn…" His fingers found my entrance. "New homework, no underwear. Ever."

My head fell back against the wall as he teased me, both with his hands and with his mouth. He deepened the kiss while I rode him, trying to find some sort of relief that felt almost impossible to get.

"Relax," he coaxed me, his mouth sliding down my neck, everything built inside me. "That's it, Kora, it's just us… use me, no guilt, no shame."

I whimpered and moved with him.

Expletives flew out of his mouth as I found my release and came apart for what seemed like the first time in years. I let out a sob as tremors wracked my body, my legs felt like jelly as I tried to lean against him. The throbbing aftershocks seemed to go on forever. I wanted more. More pressure. More of his hand. More of him, I didn't want to let go yet. With shaky hands, I held him.

Chest heaving, he stared me down his mouth swollen, slowly he pulled his hand away from me and then brought one finger to his mouth and sucked. "Better than apples…"

I gaped at him.

The door jerked open.

Slater took one look at us and then away. "Forgot my books."

"Leave." This from Leo.

Slater sniffed the air, looked at Leo, then back at me. "Five minutes, huh?"

"My fault." I grinned. "I was just giving him a recipe for apple pie."

"Ah, good call, feed the obsession." Slater shook his head and then closed the door.

Leo leaned over and whispered. "I'll eat your apple pie any day... Professor Robinson."

I knew in that moment, neither of us would ever look at another apple the same way again.

And because of that.

For the first time in what felt like years...

I laughed.

And felt it in my soul.

Chapter Fifteen

"Orgasms free the body—but a good kiss?
That can set the soul on fire.
Hah, and they say I'm not deep."
— *Leo Blackwood*

Leo

I slept like complete shit and mentally texted her about a million times. It's not even like she left on bad terms, simply grabbed her purse, gave me a finger wave, and left.

Fucking left.

I didn't give a flying shit that I was so hard that I was in physical pain—no, it was about the way she flashed me a grin I couldn't decipher.

And a finger wave?

Really?

I'd never been the sort of guy to over-analyze every single detail of an encounter. In fact, I was usually the guy with all the answers.

Instead, I woke up that next morning, sans texts and

emails from Kora, and wondered if I'd completely screwed up the fragile ground we'd built, the headway we'd made.

The guys were both still sleeping when I went to take a shower, but when I tiptoed back in the room, they both had mugs of coffee in their hands and unreadable expressions on their faces.

Honestly, it felt a hell of a lot like sneaking back in after a late night out and seeing that not one, but BOTH parents stayed up and decided to wear their disappointed faces, so much worse than the angry faces, so much worse.

"What?" I flashed them an innocent smile. "You guys are acting weirder than normal."

Finn's eyes narrowed into tiny slits. "Anything you want to… oh, I don't know…" He, swear to all that is holy, lifted an apple he'd hidden from behind his back to his mouth, and took one juicy bite.

I couldn't help my reaction.

Pure lustful thoughts about my professor.

I gulped. And immediately started to sweat. "Um, no, no I don't think so; I have class in a few though, so…" I coughed.

"Uh-huh," Slater glared at me over the rim of his coffee cup. Bold Red letters stood out against a black background, advising the world that he killed unicorns. Typical. "So, when I came back into the room last night, and it smelled like multiple orgasms, and she was wearing a look of pure bliss, it was just… your natural musk that did the trick?"

"Maybe I just have strong pheromones." I shrugged.

"Or…" Finn took another bite. "Maybe you're full of shit?"

"Shit. He's full of shit." Slater sighed. "Look, I'm all about you ending up with the girl, but you can't just…" He stopped talking and looked like he was looking for the right words. "Engage in sexual play in our dorm room, when she's still a client."

"The hell is sexual play?" I muttered.

"Don't make him draw graphic pictures bro, I'm still traumatized from last time." Finn pointed his coffee cup at me. "The point is if she's under contract—"

"—she can't be under you," Slater advised helpfully. "Or on top of you, like spooned by you, or I mean if you want to get more complicated—"

"Please no." I let out a rough exhale. "I'm sorry, but we were both consenting adults, and I just…" I was contractually screwed, wasn't I?

"You were just…" Finn lifted his coffee cup in the air. "…being a horny middle school boy with no manners?"

I glared. "I always leave my women satisfied."

"Ohhhh," Slater scoffed. "So now the client is… yours?"

"Yes," I barked. "Mine. All. Mine."

Finn shook his head slowly like he was disappointed in me. "You're like a kid who's trying to hoard all the Legos, bro."

"At least I do shit with my Legos," I fired back.

Slater frowned between the two of us. "Are we still talking about our client, or have you guys just made things weird?"

I collapsed onto my office chair and spun to face them, leaning my elbows on my thighs. "Look, I'll talk to her about terminating the contract. It's not like she hasn't improved leaps and bounds over the last two days."

"Do you hear yourself?" Finn asked. "Two days does not heal years of emotional trauma from an asshole husband. You may think you're doing her a favor, but you're swooping in when she's not ready, which means this can only end one way."

"Heartbreak," Slater finished for him.

"I won't break her heart." I rasped.

"Bro." Finn walked over and patted my shoulder. "I wasn't talking about her."

He didn't need to say anything more as he handed me his coffee mug, grabbed his shower caddy, and left the room.

"You feel the same way?" I asked Slater without looking up at him.

I could feel his sigh more than I could hear it, always was an empathetic bastard. "Look." His messy hair was pointing all over the place as he ran a free hand through it. "I want what's best for you. We aren't just friends, we're family. I just don't want you to get hurt. She's older, she wants different things. Yes, I think you should go for it because you'll regret not going for it, but remember that whole talk about the friend zone?"

"How could I forget?" I snorted out a laugh.

His smile was sad. "All right, well, we were talking about the friend zone, you just skipped right to the buffet. Nothing wrong with a little taste, but I know you, it's not gonna stop there, and she needs more than an orgasm, man."

"I know that."

"Then you have to be ready to give it to her. If you can't, walk away before one or both of you get hurt."

"I hate when you sound rational," I grumbled.

"Right?" He winked and walked past me, only to back up a few steps and ask without making eye contact. "Was it good?"

"No man." I sighed in contentment. "It was great."

He nodded and walked out of our room.

I spun back around toward my desk and fired off a text. Screw that whole you text me first rule.

> Me: Hey, want to get coffee later?
>
> Kora: I can't.

My stomach dropped.

> Me: Then why don't I bring the coffee to you this morning?
>
> Kora: I don't have class until three.

I exhaled and went for it.

> Me: Then I guess that means I'm making a delivery.
>
> Kora: I'm not ready yet.
>
> Me: Good. Stay comfortable.
>
> Kora: I'm not sure...
>
> Me: Live a little. I'll be there as soon as I can with coffee and... pastries?
>
> Kora: WHY DIDN'T YOU OFFER PASTRIES FIRST?

I barked out a hard laugh.

Me: My mistake. I'm such an amateur. Lead with sugar, always lead with sugar! IDIOT!

Kora: And you were doing so good...

Me: I've never been more ashamed in my entire life. I'll make up for it with all the carbs, and bonus they don't count because I'll bless them before I bring them into your house!

Kora: That works?

Me: Always.

Kora: Lies.

Me: Eat.

Kora: I am hungry...

My stomach growled on point.

Me: Same.

I almost typed "for you," but the previous conversation with my guys didn't exactly have me feeling good about hitting on her that hard less than twenty-four hours after tasting her.

Kora: Fine... you know where I live.

And just like that... My day was made.

Chapter Sixteen

"When all else fails—feed them.
In my opinion, women don't eat enough,
and that's ridiculous because cupcakes save lives!"
— Leo Blackwood

Kora

Crap, crap, crap, crap. I sprinted around my messy apartment, throwing away take out from last night. My dirty laundry was everywhere in my bedroom, so I dumped everything, even clothes I wasn't sure about into the basket and shoved it in the corner, made my bed, then ran into my bathroom, brushed my teeth, and tried to manage my hair.

I was just about to pull it into a tight ponytail when I remembered what the guys had said about living differently, freer, and instead pulled my hair into a loose braid over my shoulder.

I was still without any makeup and couldn't stand my tired expression in the mirror, so I added some cover up, lip gloss, and mascara. I looked like I'd semi-gotten ready but not date-worthy.

My fluffy candy cane socks were still on, but I loved them, and Stuart loved rubbing against them, so I kept them on and put on a pair of black leggings then completed the look with a gray hoody.

Good. Enough. Right?

I was sweating by the time I made it back into my own kitchen and started piling dishes into the dishwasher when the doorbell rang.

With a grin on my face, I practically sprinted toward my door and swung it open. "That was really fast, you must have—"

"What?" Chadwick's grin was cruel. "I must have what?" He shoved the door open. "Expecting company?"

I gulped and backed away from him. It was a complete habit. "How'd you get my address?"

"Don't insult me." He rolled his eyes. "Money gets you pretty much whatever you want."

Except me. He didn't get to see me. I lifted my chin in defiance as he did a small circle of my nine hundred square foot apartment.

It was small, a bit dated, but it was mine.

"Wow," he croaked. "You live here, and you still want me to sign papers?"

"Shocking. I know." I said sarcastically. "Chad, why are you here?"

His smile was manipulative. "Can't a man visit his wife?"

"No." I gritted my teeth. "And I'm not your wife. We're separated. And I thought we were meeting next week?"

He rolled his eyes. "Idiot student of yours. Is he stalking you? Do I need to turn him in to the administration?

Because that kid's been holding a torch for you since he was eighteen, asshole punk."

Kid? I wanted to argue that he was anything but.

He was a man through and through, a man who knew how to use his mouth, his hands, his hard body.

I inwardly shivered.

Compare him to Chadwick, and he was a sexual god.

"Look, I have a meeting with a friend in a few minutes. It's private. Anything that you need, you can get through our lawyers."

Chad's jaw twitched. "And the wedding? You're coming, right? As my plus-one?"

The charming smile was back, and I was so tired, so damn tired of being used, of being afraid.

Of being cornered.

My hands shook. "And I'm still thinking about it."

"What's there to think about?" He circled me; the smell of his spicy perfume made me want to vomit. I was also petrified that he was going to unravel the Burberry scarf from his neck and use it on me, tie me up, tell me it was all fun and games and then make me listen to him while he yelled obscenities at me.

It wouldn't be the first time.

His black Prada shoes clicked against my hardwood floor as he watched me through his thick black glasses.

"A lot," I finally said. "I want you to sign the papers, but how do I know you'll even do it?"

"I keep my word."

My head jerked in his direction. "Funny, I wonder what

your word meant when you hit me. Isn't there a line in your vows about protecting? Loving?"

He went still. "You were ungrateful, still are."

"I'm tired." My chin wobbled. "Please leave."

"And now you're kicking me out?" He laughed. "Ridiculous that I even came, a man like me shouldn't have to grovel, most of all to a woman like you."

Tears filled my eyes. "You're a jackass."

The back of his hand landed across my cheek so hard that I stumbled to the floor. "I'll be in touch."

And then he was gone.

I held my throbbing cheek as tears spilled onto the hardwood. I tried to stop them, but the more I tried to hold them in, the more came until I was huddled on the floor with my door still open and what makeup I'd put on completely gone.

"Kora?" Leo yelled my name. "Wow, door's open already, you weren't perchance waiting for me and—"

His hands were suddenly on me.

I let out a little yelp, and then I was in his lap. "What the hell? Who did this? What's going on? Do I need to call the police?" He started examining my head maybe looking for blood, more bruises, I couldn't find my voice enough to tell him they were mostly on the inside.

Which was a bit harder to prove in court, wasn't it?

"Sweetheart, talk to me, I'm trying not to freak out, but you aren't using words, and I see tears, and your cheek is swelling."

"He—" I found my voice as Leo rocked me, his arms like a vise around my body, holding me safe, close secure.

"He came… and things were tense but fine, and he got mad and backhanded me then left."

"Son of a bitch!" Leo snarled. Then he added enough curses to make my ears bleed. "Did he touch you anywhere else? Hurt you anywhere else?"

"N-no." I sniffled. "No, it just scared me, I was handling it okay, and then I called him an asshole."

"Good girl."

"And that pissed him off enough to hit me. He's only ever done it a few times, not hard, but he likes to corner people, and I think he just… lost it."

Leo cupped my cheeks, wiping the tears away with his thumbs, he smelled so good, his body was so warm. "What was he doing here anyway? How'd he find you?"

"Who knows how he found me?" I felt the panic rising in my chest. "He called this last week asking me to be his plus-one for a wedding. It's going to be the premier event in Seattle, and he wants something nice on his arm. He said he'd sign the final papers if I went, and I hadn't given him my answer yet."

"No." Leo clenched his jaw, breathing heavily. "The answer is no. Men like that dangle carrots then take them away. It amuses them. Fucking narcissist."

I sighed. "Then what do I do? I want to be done!"

He gave me a helpless look I felt all the way down to my soul. "We'll figure something out. In the meantime, I'm going to close and lock your door, and then I'm going to shove carbs into your body, so you feel better. That okay with you?"

I nodded weakly as he helped me to my feet and pulled out one of my kitchen chairs.

Leo moved around the apartment like a roommate, like he knew exactly where everything was, and something about his graceful movements calmed me down, maybe it was his confidence, maybe it was because he could break Chad in two if he wanted to—whatever it was—it felt good.

My door was closed.

Locked.

And then Leo was sitting across from me, opening up a bag. "Frost Donuts."

I groaned. "My favorite."

"Same." He had bought at least a dozen maybe more, of all different sizes, colors, sprinkles. "You have to eat at least one full one, trust me it will make you feel better."

You make me feel better. I didn't say it out loud, but it was on the tip of my tongue.

His eyes locked with mine as he slid his hand across the table and squeezed my fingertips, then lifted them to his lips and softly pressed a kiss to each finger with such gentleness I almost swooned into a puddle at his feet.

"Your lips," I said without thinking. "They feel so warm."

"Your fingertips are cold. I think you're still in shock." He smiled sadly. "Eat. Before I get gray hair."

I laughed at that. "Says the twenty-one-year-old."

He frowned. "I'm hurt. Did you forget I was held back? Twenty-two."

"Practically one foot in the grave," I said with an arched brow.

"It keeps me up at night, really does," he fired back. "I mean, I get these aches in my hips, scares the shit out of me. How can I please my woman if I can't even do the right—" he started rolling his hips literally in his seat like he was auditioning for Magic Mike, and I honest to God nearly dropped my donut onto the floor "—movements…"

"Er…" I gaped. "I think you're pulling it off, big guy."

"Aww…" He put a hand to his chest. "You called me big."

Heat flooded my cheeks. "I meant physically!"

"I know." He winked.

"NO!" Panic set in. "I meant as in your body, not your… penis."

He sobered and then burst out laughing. "Your blush may be my favorite thing I've ever seen," And then his eyes lowered. "It's good to have favorites, favorite things, favorite… tastes…"

"Okay." I took a deep breath. "I thought this was just coffee and donuts?"

He took a huge bite out of his maple bar and nodded, mouth full. "It's both."

"Sure…" I nibbled my donut and then reached for one of the coffees. "Black?"

He made a face. "Real men don't drink lattes."

I smirked. "Well, I'm a girl, so tell me you at least added cream?"

He scoffed. "My drink…" He took my cup. "Is black coffee." He swapped our cups. "Your drink is a white chocolate Americano with cream."

I scrunched up my nose. "Won't that be too sweet?"

"Nope." He grinned confidently and leaned back in his chair. "It brings out the espresso flavor."

I shrugged and took a sip. He was right. It was sweet but balanced out perfectly by the espresso shots and splash of cream. "I think I'm in love."

He flinched and then looked down uncomfortably at his hands. "Good. I'm hoping it's a good distraction."

He was more than a distraction; he was dangerous. "It was. It is, I mean."

"Good."

Silence descended as he watched me, and then he stood and moved behind my chair, placing his hands on my shoulders with just enough pressure that I instantly relaxed. "That feels nice."

"For the record, I'm not here to kiss you even though it may be killing me inside... I'm not here to get laid, even though I can promise you it would be the best sexual experience of your life—" I burst out laughing "—don't knock me until you try me." He dug his fingers in and massaged. "I'm here as a friend, as someone who will listen. Most of all, I'm here as a guy who's been forced to grow up way too fast, who for the last four years hasn't forgotten the first woman to make him crush so hard he was afraid he would never recover from her rejection."

"You mean Aly?"

"Kora..."

"Oh, sorry." I stared straight ahead, an amused grin on my face. "Samantha?"

"Don't make me kiss it out of you..."

"Ohhhhh, definitely Krystal. She had a thing for you and—"

In an instant, my chair was tilted back, and his mouth was on mine in an upside-down kiss. It should have felt weird, but our tongues slid against one another like hot velvet with sprinkles on top. I moaned and reached for his neck pulling him closer.

He broke the kiss shoving the chair upright, and then I was in his arms, exactly where I wanted to be as he kissed all the bad away.

I clung to his shirt.

And realized that there was no place I would rather be... than in my student's arms.

While he kissed away my pain.

Chapter Seventeen

"Awkward: See boner while licking frosting. By. Yourself."
— Leo Blackwood

Leo

I officially had a hard-on for pink sprinkles and the way they tasted on her tongue. In fact, it was all I could think about in class that next day.

Her class, to be exact.

She did a good job of acting completely normal when I was ready to scream at the top of my lungs that I'd had her naked from the waist down.

My only job yesterday was to make sure that she was distracted, that she didn't think about the fact that he'd been in her apartment, that he'd touched her. I craved to touch her everywhere, to permanently delete the bastard from her consciousness, but after our make-out session she'd said she needed to grade some papers.

And that's how we both ended up at her kitchen table, me writing a paper for her class while she smirked down at a stack of proposals from sophomore seminar and shook her head when I kept encouraging her to fail people.

A day later, and I was still concerned about her ex.

About the look on her face and the way she tried to make light of the fact that he'd touched her, but I also knew that it wasn't a battle I could fight for her.

I had learned that the hard way growing up.

It also hit so close to home that it made me uncomfortable. Did I confess everything and just hope she'd believed me?

Everyone had a past.

She wasn't proud of hers.

And it had taken me years to get over mine.

Wingmen had pulled me out of it, out of the grief, and the absolute shock over the entire situation I found myself in.

I knew firsthand that a victim had to admit that they were that—a victim—and sometimes it was easier to justify that hit than it was to point fingers and say enough.

"All right." Kora moved across the room. She was in a leather skirt again, and I could swear I felt her hips move with my hands every time the sound of her red high heels hit the floor.

Red high heels.

Damn.

It was like after our make-out session, she wanted to wear armor by way of the sexiest clothes I'd ever seen. Her blouse was black too and loosely tucked into her pencil skirt. Although she had been told to wear anything but black, to wear color, this particular black outfit could be forgiven.

My fingers itched to untuck that blouse and give it a little tug, preferably away from her body and onto the floor.

Naked. I wanted her naked.

I squirmed a bit in my seat, trying to get comfortable since my jeans were trying to chokehold my dick, and locked eyes with her as she smiled at all the students.

Me included.

I smiled back.

Knowing that her eyes had been on mine first.

"I think that's it for the day, don't forget about your senior project rough drafts! They're due next week, Thursday!"

Someone's hand shot up.

I glared.

There was always that one person who had brown all over their nose, who took notes as if there would be a dead body if they didn't cross their T's and dot their I's with a fucking heart.

I was not that person.

I judged that person.

And was currently plotting that person's death.

Jett.

Of course it was Jett.

He ironed his jeans. He told me so one day. His right eye twitched when he saw the rips in mine; it was a thing.

I learned early on not to trigger the bastard. Perfection was his middle name, and I had it on good authority that he got a B in his Kinesiology class and puked all over his professor because he was so upset.

Ah, Jett.

The puker.

"Mrs. Robinson?" His voice was deep; it didn't match his tall, lanky body, but I digress… "If we're already finished, can we just submit the rough draft?"

See? Brown noser.

Sucking up.

You don't get extra credit for being fast, you dipshit.

I held my groan in while the rest of the class started to get restless.

"Of course." Kora beamed. "If you're finished, you can submit it to the online portal, and I'll take a look at it."

"Great." His hand went down and then shot right back up.

Did he have a death wish?

The guy sitting to the right of him gripped his pencil so hard I was afraid it was going to snap in half and find the sharp end impaled in Jett's neck.

"Yes?" Kora said through clenched teeth. "What is it, Jett?"

"I'm going to assume my rough draft doesn't need much work. Can we start on our final draft if we—"

"Yes," I answered for her. "The answer is yes. If you want to work on your final, nobody's going to hover over your computer desk and arrest you. Can we be dismissed now?"

Jett scowled.

"YES!" Kora nearly shouted. "Go, go. And Jett, do whatever you think is necessary regarding your paper."

Everyone bolted.

Everyone but me.

The only thing I wanted to bolt was the door to the classroom without caring who was left inside, but since that would be frowned upon, I reached into my messenger bag and grabbed a shiny red apple, then tossed it to Kora once I made it to the front of the room. "Hungry?"

Her cheeks blushed bright red. "Brave."

"Not really. To anyone else, it's just an apple."

"Oh?" She backed into her desk; her hand held the apple out like it was poison. "And what is it to you?"

I grinned. "You really don't want me to answer that out loud, your cheeks may never recover from that blush."

She bit down on her lower lip and then put the apple on her desk and crossed her arms. "I think we need to talk about... things."

I didn't like the sound of that. No part of me rejoiced at the nervous look on her face, so I tried to turn the tables.

"Or, we could just not talk?" I offered. "I'll use my hands, mouth, possibly more food because let's be honest, I like to keep things fun—and we lock the door."

Her eyes darted toward the door then back to me, her fingers turned white as she gripped the edge of the desk. I wasn't sure if she was trying to stay in her spot or if she was stressed; either way, I didn't like it.

"Leo, look, I um, I like you a lot."

My heart slammed against my ribs in a way that felt like I was a teen again with his first crush. My breathing picked up. She liked me, she really liked me. And someone smack me. "Good," I finally breathed out.

"But."

My head snapped in her direction. *Did she just "but" me?* The worst word in the human language. But. It almost always followed good news, news that made you want to jump on the rooftops and boast.

I hated the word but.

But had no business in my life.

"But," She repeated again. "I'm… your professor and—"

"I'll drop the class," I offered quickly.

She gaped. "You won't graduate."

I flashed her an easy smile. "I'll still walk, I would only be three credits short, I'll just retake it this summer. See? Problem solved. Now can I please bite into your—"

"No." She shook her head then moved away from me, putting her massive desk between us. "I won't let you do that, it's stupid, we only have a few months until graduation anyway, right? I already decided that I was going to do one more session with you guys and then… I don't know, start rebuilding my life. And I can't do that when I'm constantly worried about losing my job."

I scowled. "We wouldn't be the first student-professor-relationship. You know that, right?"

"Right," she agreed with a sigh. "But that's not what I want."

My stomach dropped. "What do you mean?"

"A relationship." Her eyes filled with tears. "I don't want that, Leo. I can't. I can't go from one bad relationship into a whirlwind with you, I just can't."

I moved around the desk slowly. "Kora, we'd take it slow. I'm not proposing to you."

Her smile was sad as I reached for her chin and then gave up and dropped my hand to my side.

"I know that. But see, I'm already attached, and it's been a few days…"

Maybe for her.

Not for my heart.

My heart had been hers for years.

But I kept the words in.

See? *But* just kept rearing its ugly ass head.

"Don't," I whispered. "Don't push me away, not when it's already this good."

"I need to figure out me before I can even begin to figure out a way for there to be an us." She looked down. "I'm sorry."

I was good at convincing people to do anything.

I excelled at getting my way.

But I knew, in her posture, the way she turned away from me.

This was not one of those times.

"I won't give up, you know," I said. "And not because I like a challenge." I reached out to her and tilted her chin toward me. "But because you don't even realize how far gone I am for you. Call it whatever you want. I was too young then, maybe I'm too young for you now, but the heart doesn't measure its beats based on age, it doesn't say, beat slower she's eight years older, just like it doesn't say beat faster he's finally ready for you. It just is. The heart doesn't discriminate. And mine hasn't for the last four years. If you're telling me you need time, I'll wait forever. But if you're telling me that this can never happen, then I need to let you go, and I need to know now."

She opened her mouth and closed it.

Was that my answer?

I felt something lodge in my throat and swallowed down the emotion I felt raging inside.

"Leo, I just… I don't know. I can't give you that answer right now."

I dropped my hand and nodded. "I have another class."

"Okay." Tears filled her eyes.

"It shouldn't feel like this, you know…" I backed away from her. "It shouldn't feel like we're breaking up when we weren't even together. It makes you want to ask yourself the question… why?"

"Leo…" Her voice cracked.

"For the record." I pulled open the classroom door and sighed. "You look really pretty today."

A tear slid down her cheek, and I fought every impulse I had to turn around and catch it, to kiss away the one that would soon follow.

I clenched my teeth.

And I left the room.

With my heart dragging on a fucking chain behind me, hitting every single object in that hallway, bruised, bleeding, broken.

Chapter Eighteen

"Heartache feels a hell of a lot like a heart attack.
Don't confuse the two, one may be easier to fix than the other."
— Leo Blackwood

Kora

My next class went by in a blur. In fact, I was surprised I even accomplished looking half normal on the outside when my heart was trying its best to glue itself back together on the inside.

He had to know I was scared.

Not of him.

But of how strongly I already felt for him.

Leo was strong, commanding, he knew what he wanted, and he was protective and loyal. He was a girl's walking dream.

And he wanted me.

Me.

The divorced adjunct professor whose life was a mess, whose husband hadn't even signed paperwork yet.

And that was the other thing.

I was legally separated.

Not divorced.

So being with Leo still felt—like I was breaking some sort of rule even though I wasn't wearing my wedding ring, even though my ex was an entitled asshole.

I was in my office eating my turkey sandwich and staring at my computer screen, willing an email to pop up from my star student.

Nothing.

I guess I thought he'd put up a bigger fight than that.

I frowned down at my keyboard and tried to dislodge the emotion that was clogging my throat every single time I thought of him.

I had known what I was doing when I walked into class this afternoon. I wanted to impress Leo. I wanted him to see that I was listening, that I was confident, and a small part of me wanted his approval.

And I got it every single time we locked eyes.

He looked ready to jump over his desk and shove me against the wall.

I liked it too much.

And I wanted it even more.

But everything was such a mess, there were no clean lines in my life, only messy ones that were blurred together.

I put down my sandwich and refreshed my email.

Nothing.

A loud knock sounded on my door, scaring me to death.

I spun round in my chair. "Oh, hi Finn?"

"Is that a question?" He grinned, stepping his athletic

frame into my office and quietly shutting the door after himself.

He wasn't wearing the typical Wingmen uniform, but black skinny jeans and a hoody.

He almost looked normal except for the brown and blond colored hair, hypnotic eyes, and sensual smile.

How was it possible for each of the guys to just ooze sex every time they walked into a small room?

"What did you say to Leo?" He pulled out a chair and sat down, leaning his arms on his legs, creating only a foot of space between us.

I let out a rough exhale. "I just wanted to be honest with him."

Finn made a face. "Normally, I'd say yes be honest, but he came back to the dorm, slammed the door shut, and won't talk to either of us."

"He's probably processing."

"Right, but what's he processing?"

I hesitated and then, "I told him I needed time, and he said he'd wait forever, and then he asked me if I really needed time and if there was even a chance, and I told him I couldn't give him an answer."

Finn cursed. "That probably could have been handled better. Aren't you supposed to be the adultier adult?"

"Is that even a word?"

"Yes." His smile fell. "Look, your love life is your own thing, and it's really none of my business, but when it affects our business, that's when I step in, he's going to scare the shit out of our clients. He's supposed to be the sexy one they fantasize about, and right now, he's hiding under a Spiderman pillow and cursing women everywhere."

"Spiderman?"

"Don't get sidetracked."

"Sorry." I gulped. "I can't give him what he wants, Finn, not now, maybe not ever."

"I get it." He stood. "You're scared. He told me what happened, you know, with your ex at your apartment. He wanted to go to the cops, but I told him to let you handle it. I think you're scared he got in too far already, I think you're trying to undo things that have already been done, and I know without a doubt you'll regret this if you don't fix it."

I clenched my hands in my lap. "I'm his professor."

"Excuse." Finn rolled his eyes.

"I could be your... older sister!" I crossed my arms.

"Excuse number two and trust me you look more like my younger sister before she started hitting the botox because it's and I quote 'preventive.'"

I smirked. "Actually, it is." I laughed. "Finn, did Leo send you?"

"No, he'd kick my ass if he knew I was here right now."

I laughed at that. "My divorce isn't finalized yet."

"Ah, there it is, excuse number three... so get dipshit to sign the papers."

"Well, dipshit wants me to go to a wedding as his plus-one, and that's his leverage to get back into my life, so I go and he might sign, I don't go and he just prolongs this whole experience. And I don't have the money to fight him in court right now."

"Done." Finn shrugged.

"Excuse me?"

"I said done." He opened the door. "But, you'll need Leo's help."

"Leo's help for what? I think I'm confused?"

"I would do loads of groveling."

"Groveling?"

"His dad, you do know what his dad does, right?"

"No?"

"One of the best divorce lawyers in the state." Finn grinned. "Woman needs to do her research. Shit." He barked out a laugh. "You have your last session with us tomorrow night. Wear something comfortable, and I'll make sure Leo doesn't walk out of the room the minute you walk in. Talk, and then ask for help you know he's already willing to give."

"Leo thinks he knows me more than he does," I whispered. "There's so much more than—"

"I'm gonna stop you right there, that's why people date. And trust me, there's a lot to Leo that you don't know too. He's not some rich kid who's been handed everything. Things look good on the surface, but he has his demons. Funny, since his story rivals yours in a huge way, I'm surprised you don't already know about it..."

"How would I?"

"It was on the news for two weeks straight," he said, piquing my curiosity. "Tomorrow, eight. See ya, professor."

My chest ached when he said, "professor."

It reminded me of Leo calling me Mrs. Robinson.

"Wait!" I grabbed an apple out of my lunch and tossed it at Finn. "Give this to Leo for me?"

Finn scrunched up his nose. "A small part of me's

curious, the other part doesn't even want to know what this means."

I laughed. "Make sure he gets it today, okay?"

"Any, er, message you want to pass along with this titillating piece of fruit?"

"No message needed." I beamed.

"That's what I was afraid of," Finn grumbled, and then he was gone.

My office was too quiet again.

I checked my phone.

Two missed calls from Chadwick.

Of course.

Because the wedding was this weekend.

I drummed my fingertips against the table and barely kept myself from looking up Leo's name online.

It wouldn't be fair to read about his past.

Especially since I was having such a hard time with mine.

I had a decision to make when it came to that gorgeous man. And Finn was right. I was using every excuse I had to stay standing still instead of leaping into my student's arms.

Ironic.

The rest of the day went by in agonizingly slow minutes. And by the time I reached my apartment, all I wanted to do was sleep.

But when my head hit the pillow, my phone buzzed.

I quickly checked it.

> Leo: Didn't know students were eligible to receive apples. Is this a new rewards program

for star students? Or just the best-looking ones? Asking for a friend...

Tears of excitement filled my eyes.

Me: Oh, I'm sorry you were supposed to get your certificate in the mail. I'll be sure to overnight it and add a yellow star to the side for an added bonus. And of course, this stays between us. Wouldn't want the other students getting jealous of your status or your good looks.

Leo: Too late.

Me: Your arrogance is as alarming as it is cute.

Leo: OMG did you just call me cute? Hold on, I need to go tell my friends... brb.

Me: I think they already know...

Leo: Finn just gave me a high five, and I think Slater shed a small tear. We're gonna talk about it at recess later.

Me: Just as long as you're not caught passing notes in class...

Leo: The only notes I'm passing are the ones to you, I get an extra point for graphic language, correct?

Me: Only if it's paired with a solid drawing.

Leo: Don't challenge me, I may just do it to see that blush again.

Me: I'm pretty sure I've seen it all.

Leo: And I'm pretty sure you haven't...

Me: Try me.

Leo: You haven't seen all of me... but you will.

Me: Are you threatening to moon me?

Leo: I'm going to moon you backward, but in a more romantic way that has you dropping to your knees in thankfulness—just like the Pilgrims.

Me: How are you a straight-A student?

Leo: Oh, that's easy. I flirt with all my professors, including the men.

Me: REALLY?

Leo: No, only one, but she bruised my heart a bit today, so I'm texting in order to build up my courage again.

Me: I'm sorry...

Leo: I figured the apple was a peace offering of sorts.

Me: It was. It is.

Leo: Finn said he told you some things...

My heart jumped in my chest. Was he going to tell me what happened? Open up?

Me: He didn't tell me any specifics though he did tell me about your dad.

Leo: Is that why you sent the apple? Because of my dad?

Me: NO!

An unknown number has entered the conversation.

Unknown: It's Finn. It's also eleven pm. I'm exhausted. I have a class at seven, if you two don't stop text fucking I'm going to shove Leo out the window. Mrs. Robinson, I'm so disappointed in your lack of boundaries. KIDDING HAHA, but not about the Leo thing. I will kill him dead.

Leo: Unlike the rest of us, he needs his beauty sleep. And Kora, I would help you regardless of what our relationship was. Know that. Gotta run.

Me: Thank you. Sorry Finn, go sleep!

Finn: Thanks MOM! <—sorry I've been sitting on that one for dayz!!

Leo: Sigh. You should hear him laugh at himself, now THAT'S alarming. GO TO BED YOU WHORE! Not you Kora, Finn.

Finn: Tell me a bedtime story, pleeeeease.

Me: I'm with Leo on this one, you interrupted us anyways, go to bed! Wait, how did you even do that?

Leo: He shoved me off the bed, grabbed my phone, added himself in, and then grabbed his phone, and well, you can imagine, lots of cursing.

Finn: He threatened to show me his dick if I ever did that again. And now I'm scared.

Leo: He doesn't like big things.

Me: ALL RIGHT THEN, I'm just going to go sleep now!

Finn: Good thing that didn't end on an awkward note, huh?

Leo: Shut the hell up.

I smiled down at my phone.

Me: Night, boys.

I got nothing but silly emojis from both of them back and fell asleep with a smile on my face wondering when I could get Leo alone and ask him about his past and why it was so important in dealing with mine.

Chapter Nineteen

"Grand gestures are called grand for a reason.
Go big or don't let the door hit your ass on the way out."
— Leo Blackwood

Leo

"You need to tell her," Finn said for the millionth time that next evening. We were getting the room prepped for our final client of the night. The woman I wanted.

Thank God her contract would be done as of nine p.m.

At least then, I wouldn't be breaking company policy when I kissed the hell out of her and touched every smooth inch of skin.

"Tell her what?" I lit a candle in the common area and grabbed a bottle of chilled white from the fridge. Slater was the only guy in the opposite suite, which worked in our favor when we had clients.

Finn took the bottle out of my hands and uncorked it. "Your past. Don't you think it's a bit ironic?"

"Or embarrassing," I muttered.

"Hey." Finn set the wine down and tossed me the cork. "It wasn't your fault. That chick was batshit crazy, and you know it."

"Right, but she made me look like the crazy one. Those were… dark times." I gulped and squeezed the cork in my hand.

"That's why you have us." Finn offered a small smile. "You never know, it might make her feel better to know that it happens to everyone and doesn't discriminate sex, you know?"

"Yeah." I tossed the cork away. "I know. How do you even start that conversation? Hey um, even though I look really tough, my girlfriend used to beat me?"

Finn put a hand on my shoulder. "Or you could just say, let me tell you a story about a boy and a girl and a really unhappy ending that turned into finding my happily ever after."

I snorted. "Did you just make that shit up?"

"Sounded good, right?"

I held up my hand for a high five. "So smooth, bro."

"I am, after all, a professional." He hit my hand just as a knock sounded on our door.

"I'll get it." I'd like to say I walked slow, like a blind snail, toward that door. Instead, I jumped over the couch and was jerking it open within seconds. "Hey."

"Why are you out of breath?" Kora grinned up at me.

"He was doing pushups to get a pump on," Finn, the bastard, said from behind me.

"He lies, I already have a good pump." I didn't flex,

though I wanted to. "Finn's the one that has to do the extra... lifting."

I looked over my shoulder. Finn was holding up a middle finger. "Come on in, Mrs. Robinson, we're ready to fix everything..."

"For a price," I said loud enough for people to hear just in case they were speculating whether she was there for one of us or as an actual client. We'd had several professors use our services before.

This was nothing new.

The only new part was that I was falling for her.

And I hoped that she was falling for me, even if it was just a little bit.

I opened the door wide.

She stepped past me, wearing a UW sweatshirt and a pair of ripped jeans and Converse.

She looked like she was a student anyway.

All she needed was to have her face appropriately painted, and I could take her to a football game.

My heart sank.

I still missed it.

That part of me that she didn't know about, the part of me that still felt wrecked over what had happened, what I was forced to carry.

"So, what's today's lesson?" She beamed at me, her face free of makeup. A few freckles danced across her nose, and I lost all train of thought. "What?"

"You." I cupped her face without thinking. "You're beautiful."

Finn cleared his throat.

I pulled my hands away. They dangled like awkward mitts at my sides while Slater came out of the room and nodded toward us. "Ready?"

"Yeah." My voice cracked.

I so wasn't ready to watch them touch her.

But I had no choice.

If I touched her, I wouldn't stop.

Damn, I was going to need to sit on my own hands, wasn't I?

"Great, we're going to stay in the common room, more space." Slater went over to the couch while I handed Kora her wine and joined him.

Finn turned on some soft music, and I knew what was coming next. I wasn't sure if I was excited or full of dread.

"Today's lesson, your final lesson..." I took a deep breath. "...is learning to see yourself the way others see you."

"Isn't that what we've been doing?" she asked in a cute voice.

Slater smiled. "This is the finale of that training."

"Okay." She sat down on the couch. "So, what's my first step."

"Cute, she thinks she's a participant." Finn flashed her a grin. "All right, Slater, you go first."

Shit.

Slater sat down next to her and studied her, no words were said, the music played softly in the background. "Your eyes, they're clear, full of knowledge, I bet a lot of guys are intimidated by you." He grabbed her hand and held it in his. "Your skin is so soft that it's almost shocking," His thumb rubbed along her skin.

I ground my teeth.

"You're striking in a way that's both natural and sexy." He leaned in, his nose brushing her neck as he inhaled and then pressed a kiss just below her ear. "No man could look at you, touch you, and think average."

Her eyes went wide, her mouth trembled.

And then Slater stood, and Finn sat.

I started sweating.

Stage two.

Alarm bells went off in my head.

"Touch yourself," Finn encouraged.

"Excuse me?" Her eyes widened.

"Just your breasts, touch them."

"Um…"

"Relax, this isn't for our benefit." He said it gently. "Come on, give me your hand."

He struck fast, grabbing her hand and then covering it in his as he pressed it against her chest then lower until she was cupping herself with her right hand.

My fingers twitched, then gripped the couch cushion as her lips parted.

I officially hated my job.

"Good," Finn encouraged. "Now relax a bit. What do you feel?"

"Soft?"

Hell in a fucking handbasket.

"What else?" Finn kept his hand behind hers, so

technically, he wasn't touching her, but he could probably feel the heat from her skin.

"Soft and warm, I guess?"

"Kora, when a man touches a woman here." His smile was kind, which only increased my deep need to punch him, "The last thing they're thinking of is, wow her breasts are so warm."

Kora snorted out a laugh while I tried to mentally strangle him for taking such a long time. "Fine, then what are you thinking?"

"Everything," I rasped, interrupting him, as I leaned forward and watched her touch herself. "It's like all synapses are firing out of control, we feel everything at once, think everything at once. Wonder how we got so lucky, how we can keep it that way. We worry we're going to fuck up and that you're going to eventually realize we're frauds. And then we go back to feeling so damn good, because you're a beautiful, soft, confident woman, and you're allowing us the privilege to touch you. Something like that alters a guy. The right guy. It makes him want to make you feel good, it makes him want to fight the bad guys, win all the wars. It makes him better." My eyes locked in on her mouth. "So, you see, you hold all the power, Kora, right there, in the palm of your hand, and you don't even realize it. You are magnificent. Believe it. And you'll be just fine."

"And..." Finn shot me a curious look. "When the negative thoughts start to creep in..." He let go of her hand and cupped her face. "...you remember that you have something only you can offer the world, there's only one Kora Robinson. Your ex is an asshole, not because he can't see it, but because he can, and he doesn't like your light shining brighter than his."

She exhaled as a tear ran down her cheek.

Finn caught it between his fingertips. "No more of these wasted on him, got it?"

"Got it." She smiled so brightly I nearly fell out of my chair.

"Good." He stood. "Now, I'm going to be lame and give you a journal, I want you to write one good thing about yourself in it, every single day for the next two weeks, extra credit if you think of two. Combat the bad thoughts with the good statements."

He handed her a simple black moleskin and a marker.

I stood wanting like hell to kick everyone out.

Kora beamed up at Finn. "Thank you."

"You're welcome." He reached out, pulled her to her feet, and gave her a hug.

Slater followed.

And that left me.

I wanted to maul her.

I wanted to tell her she was brave.

I wanted to tell her she was beautiful.

Instead, all I did was stare.

"Okay," She eyed me again. "I guess I'll just be heading out. Thanks again everyone." A small nod in my direction. "You too, Leo."

I literally couldn't move.

It was like my feet were glued to the floor.

And when I opened my mouth, nothing came out.

"Have a good night, Kora!" Slater winked. "We really enjoyed working with you!"

"Thanks." She giggled, shot me one last look, lingered a bit by the door.

And then she was gone.

The minute it shut, a barrage of pillows came flying toward my head, and when they stopped, Slater grabbed a candlestick and held it high. "Don't tempt me bro, I'm this close!"

"What the hell!" I roared. "I didn't touch her!"

"Shit, you're stupid sometimes," Finn muttered, putting his hands on his hips. "Look, that was all very intimate. She's super vulnerable and kept looking to you for comfort. She lingered, *lingered,* dude, at the door. And you just stood there like an idiot!"

"Yeah, caught that, experienced it firsthand, thanks," I growled.

"Stop glaring at us and go!" Slater made a frantic motion with his hands. "Catch up to her, take her out for drinks, feed her, SPEAK!"

"Where the hell is a dog whistle when you need it, right?" Finn joked.

I shot them both middle fingers than jerked open the door and went on a sprint down the hall toward the stairwell.

I saw a flash of her sweatshirt go through the double doors leading into the dorm and sprinted past a handful of people who looked at me like I was psychotic.

She was on the path toward the parking lot.

Alone.

"Kora!" I yelled, "Wait!"

She stopped but didn't turn around.

When I finally reached her, I was panting and breathless. Anyone would think I hadn't worked out a day in my life; it was both panic and a serious lack of cardio. I like pretty muscles, not ones for function, sue me!

I held up a finger. "How do you walk so fast?"

She swiped a few fingertips across her cheeks and gave me a smile that was so sad my soul clenched. "Oh, you know, power walker."

"Are you crying?"

She bit down on her lip. "Maybe."

"Are you crying because of me?"

"It's stupid."

"Don't undo all the work, Kora," I reached for her, only to have her jerk away, her eyes darting around us like she was afraid we were going to get caught.

"First off, no student gives a shit." I jerked her against my chest and held her tight. "Second, I don't give a shit. Third, the faculty won't give a shit. You aren't our first client who works here, and right now I'm hugging you. I'm not kissing you even though it kills me a little inside. I'm not doing anything inappropriate. Human hugging human. Got it?"

She nodded against my chest, then said something muffled.

"What?"

"Come home with me?" Her eyelashes were wet.

I would look back on that moment a decade later and remember that one detail.

Wet eyelashes and how they seemed to glow in the darkness, how they made her look so innocent.

And mine.

So perfectly mine.

I swore in that moment I would never let her go. No matter how hard she fought, I'd fight harder.

And I'd win if it killed me.

"Yes." I kissed her forehead, my lips lingering above her skin, wanting to do so much more. "Do you want to ride with me?"

She frowned. "My car's right here."

"You're crying," I pointed out. "And my car's just right there." I pointed behind her.

She turned around. "Oh."

"Relax," I went over to my brand-new G-Wagon and opened the door, thanking God that I had my keys in my pocket along with my cell. "And get in."

"I was told to never get into strange cars. Is that a minivan?" She sniffed and then gave me a watery grin.

"Did you just call my really sick car… a minivan?"

"I would never." She grinned. "It's nice, by the way."

Her eyes roamed the soft white leather.

"That's better." I laughed and then helped her into her seat, going as far as to click her seatbelt in before kissing her on the cheek again. "Sorry, I can't help it."

"I'm glad." Her eyes fell to my mouth.

I cursed. "Save that for your apartment."

"I may fall asleep on the way there…"

I snorted out a laugh. "Yeah, I'm gonna wake you up, you've been warned."

That made her laugh as I shut her door and made the painfully aroused walk to my side of the car.

Drive.

I could drive in my condition.

I looked down and groaned.

I hurt for her.

Literally.

I carefully got into my seat, started the car, and backed up as country music filled the air.

"Hmm, didn't take you for a country music fan." She crossed her arms and stared at me out of the corner of her eyes.

"Are you saying you're not? Because I can turn this car right back around, young lady."

Her laugh was better than the music. "Actually, I'm a huge fan, I love Kane Brown."

I rolled my eyes. "All females love Kane Brown."

"He's pretty." She shrugged.

I was never buying another one of his songs again. "He's all right if you like that sort of thing."

"Is the infamous Leo Blackwood... jealous?"

"I don't do jealousy on the outside, I just have very graphic things that go on in here." I tapped my temple with my finger and suppressed a groan of near agony when she laughed again.

My hands sweated as I gripped the steering wheel and pulled onto the freeway. At least her place was close.

The minute I got onto I5, I nearly punched a hole through the steering wheel. Okay, I guess figuratively but whatever.

"Huh," She eyed all the traffic. "Must have been an accident or something?"

"Hmmmm," I drummed my fingers on the steering wheel. "I'll pull off on the next exit and take the back way."

"It's fine." Her hand was suddenly on my arm. "Actually, it's more than fine. Since we have time to kill… can I ask you something?"

I stared at her, then her hand, then back up at her. "Sure."

She nervously licked her lips and then seemed to give herself a mental pep talk as her head bobbed up and down in a small nod. "Finn said some things… about your past. He said you'd understand more than I realize…"

I immediately stiffened. "Finn needs a muzzle."

Her smile was soft as she leaned over the consul and pulled my hand from the steering wheel, and squeezed it. "Please?"

I switched lanes and then stared straight ahead, my left hand gripping the wheel like a lifeline as all the memories surfaced. Of course, we would be stuck in traffic, but at least that meant she couldn't jump out of the car. Then again, we were going slow enough she could do it backward without getting injured.

"I—" Great, now my voice was cracking. "I dated a lot in high school—"

"I'm aware."

I smirked. "All right, so I came to UW on a football scholarship." I licked my dry lips. "And I was an idiot who had no idea that football basically made you a god at this school. I loved the attention a little too much, partied way

152

too hard, and ended up getting in trouble when I puked my guts out at practice and couldn't do the drills." I still remembered the look of disappointment on my coach's face. "My coach was less than enthused. I wasn't the starting quarterback, but they were grooming me for the next year. I red-shirted my freshman year in order to get four full years of playing."

"So, what happened?"

We moved another half a mile on the road.

"He got me a tutor." Bile rose in the back of my throat. "She was extremely distracting and absolutely gorgeous but wicked smart. Not only did she help me with all of my papers, but she, er… let's just say we started hooking up on a regular basis. I didn't find out until a few weeks into our semi-relationship that she was one of the coach's daughters and had just transferred from another school."

Kora frowned and kept listening while I felt the trauma of the past making its way into the present.

"Anyway, she started getting really clingy, not the normal type of I miss you because you're my boyfriend, but like twenty missed calls in less than an hour, hundreds of threatening texts if I didn't get back to her right away. And when I finally did, I'd explain that I was in practice and every single time she didn't believe me, so I started texting her a picture when I got there and a picture when I left, I mean I really liked her, but it was like she snapped. There was so much jealousy, so much anger on her end that made absolutely no sense." I shuddered.

"Hey…" Kora put her hand on my thigh. "It's okay if you don't want to talk anymore…"

"No, I'm doing this. If it helps you, and if it helps you understand why I do what I do, why I care about you so much, why for us to move forward, talking about the past is necessary..." I took a deep breath. "She was controlling, but it was in such a manipulative way that I started feeling like the crazy one. All my teammates were obsessed with her, and in public she was the life of the party. Everyone kept telling me I was so damn lucky to have her. Beautiful, smart, rich. And loyal. Don't forget loyal, right?" I licked my lips. "One day I forgot my phone in my bag. She was waiting at the stadium in the parking lot. It was raining. She was pissed, yelling at me. In order to calm her down, I told her to get in my car." I frowned at the memory of the rain pounding my car as she climbed in her side and glared. "But when we both got in, she just started hitting me. Not—not open-handed slaps but full-on closed-fisted punches. And here's the thing: I was so shocked I didn't even know what to do. I mean, she was hitting me. I couldn't really restrain her without hurting her back. She scratched my cheek, caught me just above my left cheek, and the next morning I woke up with a black eye and bruises all up and down my arm."

Kora jerked her hand away and gasped. "Oh, God."

"It gets worse," I mumbled. "She called me that next day bawling her eyes out, saying she couldn't believe she'd acted that way. She woke up early to make my favorite breakfast and then started taking my clothes off, and that was that. I told her I forgave her, but never again."

"Did it happen again?"

"It gradually got worse. She'd apologize, and I'd think

we were okay again, I had somehow convinced myself that I loved her, that she loved me, we were just passionate, and I was clearly just not a good boyfriend, you know? It's weird, looking back I'm like what the hell was I thinking? But when you're in it, you become so used to it… My therapist calls it the frog theory. You put a frog in a pot of boiling water, and they freak, but if you slowly heat the water, you can kill them. Guess who the fucking frog was?" I snorted out a disgusted laugh.

"What made you finally break up?"

I shook my head. "I let her borrow my car one day. She came to pick me up from practice in it. We were headed to go pick hers up from the shop, and she saw a pink scrunchie on my wrist—we were wearing them for breast cancer awareness month, the entire football team—and she lost her shit." I felt my entire body tense. "She got onto the freeway and started driving like a crazy person. Weaving in and out of our lane, buzzing around other cars. All the time screaming… like this high-pitched screeching and shouting. I couldn't understand any of what she was saying. We cut cars off. I'm pretty sure at least one got run down an embankment. I kept—" Knots formed in my stomach. The cars ahead of us inched forward, and we followed. Sweat broke out across my upper lip. I concentrated on slowing my breathing. "I kept yelling for her to stop, and she just kept accelerating, yelling over me. I honestly thought I was going to die—"

Kora's sharp intake of breath had me gripping the steering wheel until my knuckles whitened, and my fingers hurt.

I forced myself to continue. "We swerved around a semi, and that forced her to slow down, but on the next corner, she rear-ended another car. I saw a blur of color in front of us, and that's all I remember. Then I woke up in the hospital with a broken leg, arm, two broken ribs, a messed-up face, and a punctured lung."

Tears filled Kora's eyes and spilled over. "You're lucky to be alive."

"I am."

"What happened to her?"

"A few broken bones, but she was able to go home that next day. My car was totaled, but when the police went to investigate, they found some prescription bottles in her bag along with muscle relaxers and a few other things. The name on the bottles wasn't hers, wasn't anyone I recognized. She claimed they were mine and that I was threatening to kill her, and she got scared, that I took the wheel, and that's why we crashed."

"She's insane!" Kora snapped. "What the hell?"

It was the first time I'd heard her curse. It at least numbed the pain a bit, I offered her a small smile. "You're sexy, you know that?"

She glared. "Keep going."

"Well, nobody believed me but my dad. Our saving grace was a nice little traffic camera that caught most of the chaos. Along with that, I had absolutely no drugs in my system at the time, and that she had elevated levels of Oxy and Adderall."

Kora winced. "Do you think that's why she was going crazy?"

"No, I think she was a classic textbook narcissist who needed professional help, and she started to self-medicate."

"What happened to her?"

I shrugged. "Her father quit his job. They transferred to Idaho, and she was put in a mental hospital for teens."

"Is she doing better?"

"I hope so," I found myself saying. "Even though she could have killed me, I can't imagine the type of pain or chaos that had to be going through her head to get to that place, you know?"

Kora was quiet as I took our exit. Finally. And made a right toward her street.

"You're a kinder person than I am," she said quietly. "I want to fight her, and I'm not a violent person."

I laughed. "Thanks for being my protector, but if I saw her, even I would run the other way. She's *craaazzzy*."

"Yeah, well." Kora crossed her arms. "What about football?"

I shook my head. "Too many bad memories. I miss it like hell, but I can't think about football without thinking about her. It messes with me up here." I tapped my head. "And I needed a fresh start. Wingmen Inc gave me that."

She nodded as I pulled into her apartment complex and killed the engine. The soft click of her seatbelt releasing filled the sudden hush, then she twisted in her seat and pinned me in a tender gaze. "I'm sorry, Leo. For what it's worth," She leaned over the console then cupped my face against her warm palms. "I think you're very brave."

I gulped, my eyes searching hers, maybe for permission, maybe for acceptance, maybe both.

"And I admire you more than you'll ever know." Our foreheads touched, and then my dream in real life lowered her head, and kissed me.

Chapter Twenty

"You should lose your entire soul and at the very least,
a sliver of your heart every single time you kiss.
If you don't have a physical reaction along with the spiritual,
then you're not with your lobster."
— Leo Blackwood

Kora

*H*is mouth was hot, his tongue slid past my parted lips, and my entire body sighed into him as he kissed me back with restraint like he was afraid to scare me away, or maybe afraid of the thick tumultuous emotions of our pasts colliding in our present.

I pulled away first, noticing how his green eyes seemed to swallow me whole with one lingering gaze. Mouth swollen, he tilted his head. "That was nice."

"I can do better."

His smile was everything. All white teeth and a small dimple near the right side of his mouth. "I wasn't aware we were having a contest."

"It's always a contest." I shrugged. "I can't help that I'm competitive."

"Too bad I always win." He patted me on the head. "Let's get you inside."

"'Kay." My arm shot out as he opened his door. "Leo?"

He turned.

"Thanks." My breath came out in a relieved huff. "For telling me your story, even though it was hard."

He locked eyes with me. "I would do anything for you."

He walked around the car and opened my door, and my heart threatened to pound right out of my chest and jump into his arms.

This guy.

I mean, really.

I didn't even know they made them like this anymore.

"You look confused." Small frown lines worked across Leo's forehead. "Something on your mind?"

I narrowed my eyes at him and jumped out of the car. "It's just strange, you're so…"

"Good looking?"

"Well yes, but—"

"Sexy—?"

"Leo!" I clenched my fists. "Stop, I'm trying to give you a compliment."

"Mmkay." He crossed his arms. "Go ahead."

I opened my mouth. Closed it. And then glared. "Well, now there's a lot of pressure."

"God, you're cute." He wrapped an arm around my shoulders and walked me to my door.

I clung to his shirt, not even realizing I was doing it

until he looked down at my fisted hand around the soft gray fabric and then winked at me. "So, what am I?"

"Well," I was on my way to being completely flustered by this guy. "I was going to say you're mature, but I may have to take that back."

"Because I tease?" He leaned against the door, his smile sexy as sin.

My heart took off again as I pointed my key at him. "Because you're arrogant."

"Arrogance and maturity can one hundred percent go hand in hand. Besides…" He leaned down and tucked my hair behind my ear. "I like to see you smile."

"Well…" I gulped.

"Let me." He grabbed my key, shoved it into the lock, and opened the door for me.

My clothes felt heavy on me.

My body was buzzing with awareness of all things Leo.

And he just had to lock the door behind us.

Lock us in.

Logically I knew he was just trying to keep me safe, but all I kept thinking was that my apartment was too small for both of us.

And that I wanted to jump him so bad it was nearly indecent.

I turned toward the kitchen at about the same time he wrapped his arms around me from behind.

I felt every hard inch of him and nearly died on the spot.

"Here's the thing…" he whispered in my ear, his lips pressing against my skin. "If you want me to leave, I'll leave and pick you up in the morning, if you want me to stay, I'll stay, and we can watch a movie, and I'll attempt to impress you with my Door Dash skills."

I smiled.

"Or, there's always the last option."

I went completely still. "What's the last option?"

He was quiet for several breaths, and then, "Ladies choice."

What he really meant was, your choice, you choose.

Choose him.

I turned in his arms. His green eyes were lit with lust, the room had a heartbeat, or maybe it was just mine, slamming *yes, yes, yes* against my chest.

I took a step out of his arms.

His hooded gaze was so dead sexy I started to shake.

I reached for the hem of my sweatshirt.

His eyes followed like he was hunting me. A slow swallow as his lips parted like he could taste my arousal in the air. And maybe… a man like Leo could.

Slowly, I lifted it over my head and dropped it to the floor. I was wearing a simple blue Victoria's Secret bra, nothing fancy, but with the look on his face, anyone might think I was already naked.

His hands twitched at his sides as I moved to my jeans and slowly flicked open the button. I touched my tongue to my lips, and his jaw clenched.

Slowly, I inched my jeans down and stepped out of them. I was naked except for my bra and my pink cheeky underwear.

"Turn around," he said in a low voice.

I turned, and then two palms were cupping my ass and squeezing.

I let out a moan I had absolutely no control over, and then his thumbs were in my panties tugging them down to my ankles, so painfully slow, I was almost embarrassed.

He was still dressed, and he was helping me—what? Striptease.

My pink panties dangled off my right ankle and dropped to the hardwood. His hands moved back to my ass, and he gripped my hips and jerked me back against him. I could feel the heat of his length pulsing through his jeans. Something so simple was driving me crazy, making my thighs quiver.

He rubbed himself against me, and then his mouth was on my neck, his hands on my breasts as he snapped my bra off.

Warm breath sent chills straight to my center of need as Leo kissed down my neck, taking small bites of my skin, soothing the same bite with his tongue before sucking on my collarbone, his hands moving down my stomach, sliding with such slowness that I clenched my teeth.

He gripped my right thigh from behind and lifted it, so my foot was on the kitchen table. Heart racing, I moaned when he inched his fingers down my lifted thigh to my core.

I jumped a foot when he touched me.

"Enjoy it," he rasped in my ear as a large finger entered, and then his other fingers pressed roughly against me. "Time for a lesson, professor."

"Oh, God," I whimpered. "I thought we…" How was he doing this? "I thought I was done…"

"A-plus…" His moments went from fast to slow, his pressure increased and then left me wanting when he decreased. "But I want to make sure you're ready… so I figured a little extra…" He pressed his fingertips against me. "…credit…" I started moving against his hand. "… would be a good idea."

"G-great idea."

I almost fell as he moved around me and dropped to his knees right in front of my lifted foot. With a gleam in his eyes, he draped my leg over his shoulder and gripped my hips. "I meant for me."

"Wh-what?"

"I needed the extra credit." He winked before his mouth replaced his hands, before spots appeared in my line of vision as his tongue flicked and sucked into oblivion.

I lasted less than a minute.

Could barely stand on two legs, let alone one as he quickly stood and picked me up only to walk us into the back bedroom and drop me onto my bed.

I bounced.

His shirt was already off.

Another bounce.

Unbuttoning jeans.

I gaped, my body still pulsing from the climax, as he shed every inch of clothing and showed me just how much he didn't need any extra credit.

Ever.

"Now's not the time for slow." He hovered over me,

kissing my mouth painfully hard as I tangled my hands into his long silky hair. It flopped to the side, covered part of his right eye, making him look even sexier as his massive body moved over me.

I must have missed the moment he grabbed a condom out of his pocket.

I stared it down. "Coincidence?"

"Never." He ripped the foil with his teeth. "I've wanted you since I was eighteen…"

I didn't need the age reminder.

His face softened. "I was a horny high schooler, give me some credit. You were, and are, one of the sexiest women I've ever seen in real life."

My entire body relaxed.

"I bought condoms the first day I saw you, and I promised myself that one day… one day you'd be mine."

"Let's hope those aren't the same ones," I joked stupidly.

He just smiled and kissed the fear out of me, kissed me so perfectly that I couldn't help but cling to his shoulders, hold on for dear life, and enjoy the way his heavy body felt against mine.

He was hot everywhere.

His movements fluid as he moved his mouth down to one of my breasts, then the other, sucking, licking.

"That feels good." I clutched my comforter in my hands.

He suddenly picked me up by the ass and pushed me back toward the top of the bed, my head resting against the pillow. "Any neighbors?"

"Yeah?" I frowned.

"Let's hope they're on vacation." He kissed me hard,

tugged my lower lip, deepened the kiss, tried angle after angle, leaving me dizzy as my body built up for another release.

He teased my entrance, only to pull back when I was ready to keep him there forever.

"Leo," I barked, opening my eyes.

His eyebrows shot up. "Yes, professor?"

For some reason, it didn't horrify me. It did the exact opposite, made me want to put on a tight little schoolgirl dress, and spank him.

My cheeks heated. "Fuck me."

"Yes—" he slammed into me "—professor."

A scream built in the back of my throat as his hips moved, the most beautiful thing I've ever seen in my life, was Leo gripping the headboard as he drove into me. Every single emotion I'd felt for years came bursting forward. This guy, him, it had been him for longer than I could remember. The way our bodies fit and moved in sync. The look on his eyes as he kissed my neck, slowing his movements just enough to taste my lips.

I wrapped a leg around him as he drove into me again and again.

My bed slammed against the wall. Hard.

"Right there." I clenched tight. "Leo, please!"

Our eyes locked. He was so deep, and then I couldn't hold back the climax that exploded between us.

His chest heaved as he pumped two more times and followed, dropping onto me. Slowly he rolled to his back and carried me on top of him.

Still connected.

Still his.

Maybe I was wrong.

Maybe I'd always been his—I just hadn't known it.

Chapter Twenty-One

"Jealousy isn't all bad,
not when it keeps the girl you love from asshats.
In fact, jealousy creates really great foreplay.
I mean… so I've heard."
— Leo Blackwood

Leo

"He can't have you."

"Huh?" Kora frowned down at me. "Who can't?"

"The ex. He can't have you. I just wanted to make sure that I was extremely clear." I put my hands behind my head and preened. "Also, we should probably send a gift next door." I made a face. "Or gifts, plural, how are you with chocolate chip cookies?"

Kora laughed. "Not the best."

"God, am I going to have to do everything?" I pretended to care when, really, I just wanted to be with her. Who the hell cared if I was doing things? I liked her. I… possibly loved her. "I'll bake them later, drop off a sorry note…"

"For all they know, we were watching TV," Kora very cutely pointed out.

I bit down on my lip to keep from laughing. "Sweetheart, you yelled, a lot, and quite loudly, I may even invest in some earplugs."

She swatted my chest. "I was in the moment."

"You told me to fuck you."

Her cheeks pinked. "I just—you were taking too long."

"Once a bossy professor always a bossy professor," I teased, gripping her by the thighs and pulling her off me. As sad as it made me, my poor dick was already telling the rest of my body that we could do this all night, and she was probably ready to kick me out of her house.

A loud meow made me freeze. "What's that?"

"Oh," She yawned. "Come here Stuart."

Something that looked like a fat naked rat jumped on the bed and gave me the creepiest look ever. "That's not a cat."

"It is! I mean, he is."

"He looks possessed. Holy shit, did he watch us all night? Without meowing once?"

Kora made a face and then shrugged. "He has an early bedtime, he was probably sleeping."

"Sleeping or watching us naked because he finally has friends who look like him?" I wondered out loud. "Shoo, Stuart, shoo!"

The cat just meowed more, jumped toward me, and then burrowed against my stomach.

I sighed.

"See, he likes you!"

I grumbled. "Fine, fine, but this means more sex, and if I catch him watching me sleep, there will be dire consequences."

She just laughed and took the cat and put him on the floor while I quickly went toward the bathroom, door open, and was shocked as hell when she walked past me naked as if it was normal.

I groaned.

She turned around. "What?"

"You can't just walk around like that and expect me to be good."

With a wink, she shrugged. "Who said anything about good?"

The bathroom door closed in my face.

I banged my head against it twice and shook my head as I slowly made it back to the bed and grabbed my jeans.

She opened the bathroom door, walked past me naked again. And well, honestly, she wasn't learning, I grabbed her by the hand and pulled her onto the bed again. "Do you have a listening problem, professor?"

She burst out laughing. "No, I was going to find my clothes."

"I burned them," I said somberly. "All the clothes. Gone. These things happen."

"Oh?"

"All the time."

"Oh, so the fire picks what it's going to burn?"

"It's science." I tapped my head. "Trust the star student, mmkay?" I slapped her on the ass. "No clothes for you."

She wiggled against me, probably trying to get free,

which only made me want to keep her more. "You have jeans on."

"Give me another two seconds, and I'll have them off."

"How can you—?" She went completely red.

I sat up with her in my lap. "Lesson time, you ready?"

She rolled her eyes.

I kept going anyways.

"I'm young, which means when you look at me wrong, I'm already semi-hard and trying like hell to make sure you don't notice, all right? Give me thirty minutes, and I'll show you how to properly use that kitchen table."

Her eyes widened. "Leo…"

"Yes?"

"Okay."

I nearly gave myself whiplash. "I'm sorry, what?"

"Thirty minutes, I'm going to time you. And if you can… then you may get rewarded. You're the one who likes all the extra credit…"

I closed my eyes and mumbled a prayer.

"Are you… are you praying?"

"Just saying thanks." I grinned and helped her to her feet. "Now, if we're going to do this, I need hydration."

I felt her gaze on my ass as I walked into her kitchen and grabbed a drink of water.

And I felt her presence when she walked behind me, rummaged in the cupboard only to return with two wine glasses and a bottle.

"Does this mean I'm staying?" I asked, staring straight ahead while she worked around me.

"Yes." She wrapped her arms around my middle, and a

part of my heart squeezed painfully, as my brain whispered *finally...*

Chapter Twenty-Two

*"The only way to party? The sexy slumber party way—
with snacks—the kind you lick off each other's bodies.
I'll never look at skittles the same. Use your imagination."*
— Leo Blackwood

Kora

He stayed over.

It was the sexiest slumber party of my life.

I'd never had that in my life, the laughter before, during, after sex, the easy conversation, the teasing.

It felt so natural with Leo like we'd been dating for years. And he made me feel confident, sexy. It helped that he couldn't keep his hands off of me, not that I was winning any medals for self-restraint.

I woke up with a smile on my face.

Which should have been my first clue that something was about to go wrong.

"Morning." Leo flipped me onto my back and started kissing his way down my neck until he rested his head between my breasts and looked up at me with the most adorable face. His dirty blond hair was all over the place, his eyes heavy with sleep, his mouth swollen from all of our kissing.

"You look good there." I threaded my fingers through his thick hair. "I think I could get used to it."

Both of his hands reached for my breasts and squeezed. "Sorry I couldn't help it. They exist; my hands exist. It's simple math."

"Math, science, do you always bring the classroom into the bedroom, or am I just special?"

He winked. "Only you…"

"Wow."

"I was just thinking that, but probably for an entirely different reason." He turned his head to the side and swirled his tongue around one nipple, only to sigh. "Can we stay in bed all day?"

"We have class. Don't you have a paper due?"

"Why yes, Mom," he said in a polite tone. "I do."

"Never." I jabbed a finger in his face. "Ever." I flicked his nose. "Call me your mom."

He burst out laughing. "Trust me, my mom looks nothing like you. Oh, and she has like twenty years on you, so I think you're safe."

She frowned. "How old was she when she had you."

"Aw, is my professor struggling with the math? Do you need me to do the subtracting and adding for your delicate—?"

I grabbed a pillow and slammed it into his face even though he didn't stop laughing until he rolled off me and pulled me onto his lap, his very aroused lap.

What was I pissed about again?

"Mmmm..." Leo put his hands behind his head. "Ride me."

"What?" My cheeks burned even though we'd had sex at least three times, maybe four if you counted the shower at three a.m., but that was more... well, I wasn't really sure, but it was like water gymnastics.

He gripped my ass. "You heard me... use my body, ride me, do your thing, I just want to watch you come apart before breakfast."

I pressed a finger to his mouth. He grabbed it and kissed the tip.

"Shhh," I warned.

"Who's going to hear us? The wallpaper?" His eyebrows shot up. "Ohhhh, still worried about those pesky neighbors who pounded back against the wall last night?"

I covered my face with my hands. "That was so bad."

"No, it was sooo good," he moaned. "Remember. You said so over and over and over and over—"

"Let's just not talk." I glared, even though my body was already responding to him. How could it not? I was straddling male perfection, and he wanted me.

Me!

"Agreed." He sighed and then moved his hips. "Come on, Kora... breakfast will taste so much better..."

"Are you always like this?" I truly wondered out loud.

"I can honestly say I have never been like this with anyone but you." He sobered and then leaned up on his elbows and captured my mouth with his.

I moaned, twisting my hands in his hair as I moved up

and impaled myself on him, slowly riding him the way I wanted to, holding onto his head like I was leading a horse or something.

My release was so fast that I was disappointed.

He chuckled against my mouth. "Are you frowning right now?"

"That was too fast."

"That was your fault." He tugged my lip and winked. "Also, it's morning, and we were both primed with all that school talk."

"You're impossible." I laughed and moved off him.

"And you love it..." He hopped out of bed. "Go take a shower. I'll make breakfast since someone's afraid to skip school..."

I slapped him on the ass. "Sorry, slipped."

He charged after me, but I slammed the bathroom door in his face only to have him curse about getting me back.

My smile was so wide in the shower I choked on the water as it spurted onto my face.

You'd think it would deter my smile at least a bit.

It didn't.

I quickly dried myself, put on some makeup, so I didn't look like I was up all night having sex and let out a little scream when the steam cleared from my bathroom mirror.

The door jerked open. "What? What's wrong?" Leo looked panicked.

Wordless, I pointed to my neck.

"Your neck hurts?"

"Leo!" I hissed. "I have a hickey!"

His face broke out into a grin. "And you screamed to say thank you?"

I glared through the mirror, and his smile fell. "How do I explain this?"

With a chuckle that made me want to smack him, he walked into the bathroom, he was wearing his jeans from the night before but no shirt. He was warm as he wrapped his arms around me and stared at me through the mirror. "Relax, it's not like I signed it, from your student Leo."

I scrunched up my nose. "I guess not."

"Hmm," He rested his chin on my head. "Would it make you feel better if I started a rumor that you and Professor Cunningham got busy during happy hour at Applebee's last night and had one wild moment behind the dumpsters?"

I gaped. "Cunningham?"

He pressed his lips together like he was trying not to laugh.

"The one with the toupee?"

"Hey, it looks real!" Leo defended him.

I closed my eyes and shook my head. "Spread that around the school, and I'm going to say you have herpes."

His jaw fell. "You wouldn't."

"I would." I grinned triumphantly.

"Fine." He kissed the top of my head. "Guess the hickey's mine than… sorry not sorry…"

And off he went.

I blew out an exasperated breath.

I could wear a cute turtleneck dress.

It was black, but it would have to do. I could pair it

with some over-the knee-boots and a jacket, then wear a scarf for good measure, right?

Right.

Totally fine.

I quickly put on my bathrobe and went into the kitchen.

The smell of cooking eggs filled the house, and winding its way along with that—praise the morning gods—fresh coffee.

"Wow, such good service. Should I give you five stars on the Wingmen App?" I teased.

He dropped the spatula and then glared at me. "Don't you dare."

"A-plus in bed, the best I've ever had—"

"Wingmen doesn't do house calls." His smile fell. "I'll quit."

"Wait, what?" I panicked. "I was teasing!"

"I know…" He shrugged like it wasn't a big deal, but it was. It was his job! His income. His future. "But I don't feel right lying to the owners, Ian and Lex. I'll go into the offices later this week and let them know—"

"Know what?" I said quickly.

He gave me a soft smile. "That I'm off the market and can no longer work for an app that says I have to touch another woman when I already have one."

My heart swelled even though I was still worried. "What are you… saying?"

"I'm saying I want you to be mine. And if you make me say anything else, I'll make this the cheesiest day of your life and ask you to be my girlfriend, which just makes things weird when you're an adult, right?"

"Or romantic?"

Leo sighed then dropped to his knee. "Be my girlfriend, Professor Robinson? Punish me every day when I don't—"

"Yeah, get up," I said quickly.

"Thought so." He winked and then flipped the omelet. "This one is yours… and your coffee is already waiting right there."

Chadwick had never cooked for me.

He was always in a rush and got angry whenever I left dishes in the sink because I had to hurry to school.

I frowned.

Now that I thought about it, he hadn't ever made me dinner either. We went out to the best restaurants, but he never physically did anything just for me.

Eggs. So simple. Yet it said so much about Leo. About the type of guy he was.

My stomach erupted into butterflies as he flipped the omelet onto a plate and handed me a fork.

I took it, set it down, then dropped my bathrobe to the floor. His jaw soon followed, or at least it seemed like it. "Is this what I get whenever I cook because I'll become a kitchen savant if you show me boob every time."

"You're easy." I giggled.

"No, I'm hard, soooo hard." He dipped his head for a kiss just as the doorbell rang.

"Huh." I put on my bathrobe. "I hope it's not the neighbors."

"I'll just hide." Leo flashed me a grin. "Then they'll think you were just pleasuring yourself all night."

I rolled my eyes. "You stay there, less talking."

"Yes, ma'am." He went about making another omelet.

I looked through my peephole and didn't see anything. Assuming it was a package delivery, I opened the door a crack only to have it violently shoved the rest of the way open.

Chadwick barged in like he owned the place with a little blue Tiffany's bag in his hand. "Look, I know things ended badly, but—" He frowned and took in my bathrobe, then his eyes roamed over my face, stopping at my neck, right at the hickey Leo had given me. I didn't want to bring more attention to it, so I pretended like it wasn't there. "What the hell is that?"

"Curling iron burn," I said softly. "You need to go."

"The hell it is!" He shoved past me and stalked right into the kitchen where a shirtless and unsuspecting Leo was still cooking.

The minute Leo saw him, his eyes narrowed. "Hey man, I don't remember inviting you for breakfast. You'll have to call next time, all out of eggs."

"What the hell is this bullshit?" Chadwick roared. "How long has this been going on? You went out behind my back when he was in high school too?"

"Chad—"

"You whore!"

Leo moved so fast that one minute he was behind the counter; the next, he had Chadwick by the throat, legs dangling midair. "I'd choose your next words carefully." He set him back down on his feet.

Chadwick's face turned a shade of purple. "I'm not

signing shit. You're not *getting* shit either!" He jabbed a finger at me. "I'm going to destroy you. Both of you!"

My heart cracked in my chest and fell to the floor in a thousand pieces. He always ruined everything. He would ruin the best thing that had ever happened to me.

"I'll quit," I said softly. "Before you can tell anyone."

"You think I'm going to the dean?" His laugh was ugly. "Honey, I'm going to the police to report you for fucking an underage teen four years ago, and then I'm going to the news."

"It's not true!" I yelled.

"Does it really matter?" He looked around. "It's true now."

"I wouldn't," Leo said in a deathly cold voice.

"Do you have any idea who I am?" Chadwick said in the haughty tone I was so used to.

Leo actually smiled. "Do you... know who *I* am?"

Chadwick snorted. "A punk kid who wants an easy piece of ass."

"She's anything but easy. You should know, bet she wouldn't even fuck you when you begged," Leo snapped and then shot me an apologetic look.

"I'm leaving, you'll be hearing from my lawyer, but most likely you'll see it on TV before anything else. I hope they arrest your ass."

My body swayed. This couldn't be happening.

Not now.

Not when everything was perfect.

Tears blurred my line of vision. "Chadwick, you can't do this, you can't!

He looked between Leo and me and then sighed. "Agree to come to the wedding, and I'll think about it."

"Fine," I said quickly.

"No," Leo interrupted. "This ends right now. No more manipulating."

Tears streamed down my cheeks. "Leo, please…"

"Walk away." Chadwick sneered at Leo. "She doesn't want you here anyway. Can't you tell she's upset? What sort of magic dick do you have that you'd take a married woman anyway?"

Leo's eyes flashed with hatred. "Kora—"

"Go Leo, let me handle this."

He shook his head slowly. "You're not safe. I'm not going to just leave you alone with him."

"Please." Chadwick rolled his eyes. "She's my wife. I would never hurt her."

Pain lanced through my chest. "Separated, and you agreed to sign the papers if I went to the wedding."

"That was before I found out about this little…" He looked to Leo. "Problem."

"Leo…" I was ready to get down on my hands and knees; he was just going to make it worse, other people being involved always made it worse. "Just go."

"Yeah, let the grownups talk." Chadwick crossed his arms.

"Kora, think about this." Leo pleaded. "Really think."

"I am." I clenched my fists. "You need to leave. Now."

I'd never witnessed someone's heart break in front of my eyes. I had felt it more times than I'd ever admit, but to actually see it happen… never.

I wondered in that moment, as Leo's face fell, as he went completely rigid and with jerky movements grabbed his shirt off the floor, his keys, his cell phone.

Was it more painful to experience it? Or to be the reason it was happening to someone else?

I was protecting him.

He had to see that!

This was my choice.

My mistake.

He had a future.

A bright one.

One that didn't include baggage and threats.

One that didn't include a man who could ruin him.

I only hoped one day he'd understand that I was doing everything I could to make sure he was safe, even if it hurt me.

Even if it made me want to vomit.

Even if it killed me.

Leo Blackwood, my savior, would be safe.

Leo shoved past Chadwick, knocking him back a step.

"Mature." Chadwick snorted.

"I tripped." Leo shrugged and then stopped in front of me, his eyes saying more than his words ever would as he stepped around me and actually left.

I wanted to crumple to the shiny hardwood floor in tears.

I wanted to pound my fists into Chadwick's face for taking away something so good for making me choose.

Instead, I kept my posture stiff as he dangled the

Tiffany's bag like he had countless times before and smiled. "I think we should match for the wedding, don't you?"

Chapter Twenty-Three

"When all else fails. You fight until the bitter end.
And when pigs do actually fly—you call Dad."
— Leo Blackwood

Leo

I didn't leave.

I wasn't an idiot.

I stayed in the parking lot with my cell gripped in my hand, waiting to see if I needed to call the cops. I was going to give him twenty minutes and then I was going back up there to make sure she was safe.

Leave? Her? With an abusive husband?

Was she insane?

And what the hell sort of person did she think I was?

I wanted to believe she thought she was doing the right thing.

That I wasn't just some boy toy she needed in order to let off some steam, or worse, some guy who made her feel good.

It was more than that. Deeper.

Hell, I was her boyfriend, right?

Or so I thought.

If that piece of shit thought he could mess with her or with me, he was sorely mistaken.

Besides, he seemed to think he was above the law because he had money, he had no idea that my family had more.

That I probably had more than he did.

Nor was he aware of who my family was.

I smiled. Soon he'd be the one shitting himself, and I'd find great joy in being the one to deliver the final blow.

An agonizing few minutes later, he left the apartment. His clothes weren't in disarray, and he looked happy as he got on his cell phone. I was just getting ready to go back up when she followed and dialed something on her phone then waited.

An Uber showed up minutes later.

She was wearing dark sunglasses and clothes that, while beautiful, were all black like she was in mourning.

She didn't even look up to see if I'd stayed.

I was about to get out of the car and announce myself, but she was already leaving, gone.

Just like that.

With a sigh, I drummed my fingertips against the steering wheel, then grabbed my cell and dialed.

"Leo? Are you okay?"

"Hey, Dad." I sighed. "It's a very, very long story."

"Lunch?"

I exhaled in relief. "I was thinking more a late breakfast where they serve alcohol, but sure..."

He cursed. "Are you safe?"

"I'm safe. I'm fine. It's not me, it's my..." I let out another long sigh. "It's my girlfriend."

He was dead silent and then. "It's not the same—"

"No, no." I shook my head as if he could see me. "God, no. This woman... she's my girlfriend, and I love—" Whoa, where did that come from? "I like her, love her, I don't know, Dad. She's important to me, and I know she's in trouble. This asshat Chadwick Robinson is—"

"Robinson, you say?" He chuckled.

"His last name isn't that funny."

"Oh no, but the situation is. I'll tell you at lunch, I'm sure this is about to get very interesting."

"I just hope you can help."

"They don't call me Magic Mel for nothing!"

I groaned. "Dad, enough with the nicknames."

"The reporters love it!"

"Mom hates it."

"Sometimes, I make her call me that when—"

"La la la la I can't hear you, and YES your children are all painfully aware of the times you make her do that. In fact, my ears are still bleeding. Where do you want to meet?" I checked the time. "University Village, we can get pasta or some shit."

"Hmm, tough choice."

"Dad," I groaned.

"See you in fifteen?"

"Perfect."

I hung up, feeling a bit better, mainly because my dad was a fucking badass that put the fear of God in most people—and because he was the wisest man I knew.

It also helped that he golfed with the mayor.

And that he was the newly elected, as of last year, Washington State Governor.

Chapter Twenty-Four

"Absence just pisses the heart the hell off."
— *Leo Blackwood*

Kora

Leo wasn't in class.

I hated it.

Hated that I didn't see his smiling face.

The wedding was this upcoming weekend, which meant I wouldn't see him until after I went with Chadwick, if I went. I still prayed I would find a way out of it.

I taught three classes with thick tears getting stuck in the back of my throat. It hurt to even smile.

And I hated that.

I hated that I let someone take that power from me, so I had to keep telling myself it was for the best.

I was saving Leo.

I was making sure he had a future that didn't include a possible lawsuit or other legal action over something that never even happened.

Besides, he was eighteen when I transferred to that school!

I knew it.

He knew it.

But speculation was everything, and I knew how easily Chadwick could spin things. Besides, he had the money to do whatever he wanted, and his father doted on him like he was the next messiah; at least that's what I'd always seen on the surface.

My final class ended, and still no texts from Leo even though I'd sent him a text letting him know I was safe and had taken an Uber to my car.

I followed that one with, "I'm sorry, let's talk later."

And he still didn't say anything.

I'd hurt him.

In his eyes, I had probably chosen my abusive ex over him, which was so far from the truth that I wanted to scream.

Maybe this was why we never should have gotten involved.

Both of us were hurt over different situations in our pasts, and maybe he was too young to get it. He'd never been married before, he didn't understand.

With a sigh, I grabbed my stuff, and in one last-ditch effort, made the trek to the dorm hoping to get a chance to talk with him.

I took the stairs and all too soon I was in front of their room.

I knocked once.

The door flew open.

Slater grinned down at me. "To what do I owe the pleasure?"

I opened my mouth to say something—anything really. And burst into tears.

"Whoa, whoa, whoa." Slater pulled me into his arms and shut the door so quickly my head spun.

More arms wrapped around me until I was in a Finn and Slater sandwich.

These guys.

I sniffled suddenly hot. "I'm s-sorry."

"This about Leo?" Finn asked in a curious voice.

I looked up at him. "Is he here? Can I talk to him?"

"Sorry." Finn looked apologetic but weird, like he was hiding something.

"Can I wait here until he gets out of class?"

Finn and Slater shared a look.

Slater spoke first. "He's out of all the classes. He's going to test out of his final communications class, and he somehow managed to convince the Dean of the Business Department to bypass his Senior Seminar credit based on his experience with Wingmen."

My stomach dropped. "So, he's... not in school."

"Technically, he's done," Slater said slowly. "His last year was kind of a fun year, and he was toying with the idea of taking on another minor but never got around to it since we lost one of our other Wingmen to graduation. We've been training some replacements, but they aren't ready yet."

My head was about to explode as I moved around them and sat on the couch, tears in my eyes, my heart heavy. "So, he's gone... h-he left?"

"School. Not the planet," Finn said with a smile. "He said he had a lot of things to get done today and then something about murder, which I'm hoping had nothing to do with you, but other than that, he just seemed... determined... not upset..." Finn gulped. "I'm guessing you're upset because of this morning?"

"He told you?"

"He punched a hole in our wall," Slater said in a factual voice. "So, we kind of had to know why he was destroying school property, yeah."

A lone tear ran down my cheek. "He doesn't see it now, but I'm trying to protect him. My ex, he isn't a nice man, and he said some things, made some accusations."

"You should know," Finn said softly, "Leo waited outside your apartment to make sure you were safe. That doesn't seem like the sort of guy who's just giving up."

"Text him," Slater encouraged.

"I did."

"Call him," Finn added.

"It goes straight to voicemail."

"Then, I guess you do what mere mortals are forced to do every time the person we love is hurting..."

My head snapped up.

Love?

Did I love him?

Damn tears!

I squeezed my eyes shut. "What's that?"

Finn wrapped an arm around my shoulders. "You wait for him. You wait until he comes to you."

"And if he doesn't?"

"Should we show her the size of the hole? Just so she understands the passion and anger from our young Leo?" Slater joked. "Trust me, if a man punches a hole, he's not going to be crying into his Cheerios. He's out for blood."

"Great, he's going to get himself into trouble."

"Doubtful," Finn said with a sloppy grin. "You really should research your boyfriend more..."

I rolled my eyes. "I know. I know his dad. Best divorce lawyer, but this is beyond that now, guys. The things Chadwick said—"

"Eeew." Slater made a face. "That's Dickweed's name? God, I bet he wears sweater vests."

I didn't have to answer. I'm sure my face said it all.

Both guys fell into fits of laughter.

And then Finn was getting up and pouring me a glass of wine.

"Oh no, that's okay. I'm not a client anymore. I'm—"

"Our best friend's girlfriend," Slater finished. "So yes, we do have to wine you, it's bro code. Now sit and decide if you want The Proposal or Sleepless in Seattle."

"Damn, you're good," I muttered.

"We know," they said in unison.

And that was how I found myself sitting between my boyfriend's hot best friends, drinking wine and watching chick flicks, wondering when my phone was going to buzz, and where the hell the man I cared about was.

Chapter Twenty-Five

"Always do it in person. Whatever it is.
You owe it to the person you love, even if that person's you—
hey nothing wrong with having a solid pep talk
in front of the mirror!"
— Leo Blackwood

Leo

I saw the texts.

I saw the missed calls.

I listened to the voicemails with a tight chest and had to keep myself from calling and texting.

It had been two days.

Two days without sleep while I tried to get everything ready for her. Because the thing about Kora? She wanted to save me, to protect me, but when had anyone in her life ever done the same for her?

It was my turn.

And I wasn't going to screw up my grand gesture just because my pride was a bit bruised right along with my ego.

What we had was special, it was different, and I wanted

to keep it forever, which meant, I couldn't tell her what I was doing. She'd tell me to stop, she'd get pissed, and she'd probably tell me I was being immature and rash. But I wasn't.

"You ready?" My dad asked as we pulled up to Bell Harbor near Pier 66. It was a popular event center and was right on the water.

"As ready as I'll ever be." I tugged at the bowtie. I was in a head-to-toe black tux that cost more than some people's rent. My dad had chosen black and white with a red tie because he was out for blood—voters assumed it was because he was patriotic; then again, they didn't know how ruthless a Blackwood could be.

They were about to find out.

I opened the door to the Rolls and got out while Dad tossed the keys to the valet and gave him a wide smile.

We walked in together.

I had the papers in a black leather portfolio, I was clutching them in my right hand. At this point, the wedding was over, and the reception was starting.

The lights were low as music pumped through the speaker system, Lizzo, perfect. The happy couple was already on the dance floor surrounded by friends and family as purple and white lights flashed like they were at a club.

Around twenty round tables had been placed about the room, and each one had an ice sculpture of the couple on it.

"A bit of overkill," I muttered under my breath, earning a laugh from my dad.

I scanned the crowd again and saw her.

She was sitting alone at one of the tables. Where the hell was the jackass?

"Bingo." Dad grinned. "Looks like he's talking to Fred."

"Fred?" I frowned. "Who the hell is Fred?"

"Oh sorry, Frederick, the DA. You know, Fred?"

I rolled my eyes. "I grew up calling him Uncle Freddie. How the hell would I know that you called him Fred outside the house?"

Dad grinned. "Go get the girl. I'll join you shortly."

"Right, just walk over there and get the girl, easy." I took a deep breath.

"If necessary, just kiss her." Dad nodded solemnly. "Worked on your mom."

"Pretty sure I might get slapped."

"I did." He grinned. "Worth it."

"I'm sure." I patted him on the back then weaved my way through the crowd. I pulled out a chair and sat.

Kora didn't look up for a few seconds. She was probably expecting a stranger, not her boyfriend.

At least I hoped I was still her boyfriend.

Finally, she gazed up. "You."

"Me." I grinned. "You don't mind if I steal this?" I grabbed her wine and tossed it back then set the glass back on the table, empty.

"You sip that." An eyebrow arched up.

God, even her eyebrows were perfect.

I was so gone, wasn't I?

"Yeah well, I was nervous." I leaned forward, still gripping the portfolio. "I'm sorry for not texting or calling back, but I was afraid you'd tell me not to get involved or not to drop out of school early."

She glared. "You just… left!"

"I'm right here," I said softly. "And I had a few things to get in order before I could come at you with an offer."

"An offer?" She frowned. "What are you talking about? This isn't a merger."

"No." I grabbed her delicate hand. "It's not a merger, it's your life, and I'm going to work like hell to make sure you have one."

Her eyes filled with tears. "You can't. I wish you could save me from this, but you can't Leo. He's too powerful. If I just do what he says, then—"

"He was never going to sign," I interrupted. "I talked to his lawyer, who just happens to be friends with my dad. Chadwick keeps canceling their meetings."

"But he said he was going in Monday."

"His lawyer's on vacation starting yesterday." I shrugged. "Which meant I had to work fast to get this." I opened the portfolio.

"What's that?"

"Your divorce papers." I grinned. "Just waiting for a signature."

"What?" She jumped to her feet. "But how? Why do you even have those? I don't understand!"

"You." A deep voice said behind me. "You weren't invited."

I turned. "Hello, little Chad-dick, how's it going? God, you're even shorter than I remember…" I shook my head. "You know what they say about short guys…"

"Leave," he said through clenched teeth.

"But I love a good wedding, and I know the bride." I waved over his shoulder toward the bride, who I did, in fact know, since she used to babysit me when I was younger, not that she was much older. She may have also been my first kiss. Shhh, don't tell Dad.

Chadwick glared. "You have some nerve."

"I have loads of nerves. So do you. A human foot alone has over seventy-two hundred nerve endings—learned that in school." I winked while the glower on his face said he was about ready to strangle me.

"Go before this gets ugly, not just for her but for you." Chadwick laid a possessive hand on Kora's shoulder.

Her eyes pleaded with me.

"Not until you sign the papers. That was, after all, the agreement, right?"

"Do you have a listening problem?" Chadwick snapped, his fingers digging into Kora's shoulder. "Do you really think I won't follow through with reporting Kora to the authorities? To the news? The Dean?"

"Ah, Chadwick Robinson." My dad arrived right on time, Uncle Freddie by his side, and a man I didn't recognize. "I was just chatting with your father."

"Governor." Chadwick grinned like he was winning at life. "It's an honor to see you again."

Oh, this really was the best day, wasn't it?

"I wish I could say the same," My dad said as his smile fell. "I see that you've met my son."

Aw, little Chad-dick looked like he'd swallowed a

melon, his face went completely pale while Kora's eyes went so wide, I wanted to laugh.

"We were just talking about school." I grinned wide.

"Ah, he's at the top of his class, graduating early and already has a job set up at Wingmen Inc Corporate. Then again, my Leo's been investing since he was sixteen, has a mind for numbers." I just shrugged while my dad kept talking. "Anyway, we're not here to talk about my son's many successes."

I almost repeated the word "many" to Chadwick but refrained and winked at my girlfriend instead, who was looking between us with narrowed eyes like she was trying to put two and two together.

"You're lucky," another man said as he approached. The same man I'd met with yesterday, Earl. He was a bit taller than Chadwick and had thick black-rimmed glasses. "That your boy goes after what he wants without cutting corners." He glanced at Chadwick. "Something you wanna tell me, son?"

Earl, AKA Chadwick's dad, had timed his appearance perfectly.

I crossed my arms and watched the show.

Chadwick sputtered. "N-no, I was just having a private moment with my wife."

"Ex-wife." I gave out another wide grin. "Isn't that right, Kora?"

"Yes." She reached for the portfolio and opened it. "Anyone have a pen?"

Both my dad and Earl offered one.

She took my dad's, he was closer and handed it to Chadwick. "Sign."

He cursed under his breath and hurried through the stack of papers and then got to the very end. "This isn't right."

"Oh, it's right," I said smoothly. "After all, my dad looked over every single inch."

"You were going to leave her with nothing!" Chadwick's dad hissed out. "So not only are you cheap, but Mel tells me you were threatening his son. Do you know how this makes us look? How this makes me look? The company?"

I nodded innocently.

"Dad, I—" Chadwick stopped talking and took a deep breath. "This isn't the best place to discuss personal matters."

"I think a wedding's a lovely place to get personal." Still grinning, I looked up at my dad. "Should I tell him, Dad, or should you?"

"It's your company. You tell him." He patted me on the shoulder.

"Not only are you giving her half of your assets, as per the original documents." I leaned forward, twisting my grin into a lopsided smug smile. "But as of yesterday, I own Robinson Storage." The exact company where Chadwick worked as CEO. "But don't worry, I'll let you keep your job. I'm a very generous owner." I shrugged at Kora. "It's good to diversify your portfolio."

"B-but you're a kid!" he screeched. "What did you do? Take a loan from your father!"

"He didn't need to," Earl spat. "You know we were looking for someone to buy us out after last year's loss. Leo made us an offer we couldn't refuse."

I just kept smiling and acknowledged my dad's wink with a nod.

"You have one more place to sign." I pointed at the papers enjoying the increasing shaking in Chadwick's hand. Slowly he scribbled his name on the dotted line. I stood and leaned in, so only he could hear me. "Next time, know your opponent before opening your mouth. Hopefully, this is a good lesson, chin up, you're still young."

I grabbed the portfolio and handed it over to my dad, and then held out my hand to Kora. "Shall we?"

Tears filled her eyes. "We shall."

I gripped her hand and led her onto the dance floor just as John Legend came over the speakers.

"Did that just happen?" She pulled away from me and smiled. "I mean seriously?"

"Seriously." We touched foreheads. "I'm sorry for all the secrecy, but I wanted to surprise you. Also, I had to work my ass off to get everything done in time."

"B-but why? You didn't have to—"

"The proper thing to say is 'thank you, Leo, for being my hero,'" I whispered.

"Thank you." Her voice went hoarse. "For being my hero." Her eyes darted to my mouth. "Why would you do that for me, though? Why would you go to all that trouble? Quitting school? Buying out the company?"

"I figured it would be a good wedding present." I shot her a cheeky grin. "Don't panic. I'm not proposing. After all, you did just finalize your divorce. I was thinking of dating you for, oh I don't know, a few months, then popping the question over breakfast. Eggs would have been our first real meal together, you know."

Tears streamed down her cheeks.

I drew her just a little deeper into my embrace. "You may think it's too soon, but I've loved you since the first day you walked into my classroom and told me to shut my trap."

She laughed and wiped the tears from her cheeks. "I was so nervous, and then I felt horrible that I yelled at you."

"I liked it," I whispered. "I liked you. I still like you. I told myself I would marry you one day, and then you wrote Mrs. on the board, and my soul was crushed."

She wrapped her arms around my neck. "I'm Miss now."

"You'll be Mrs. again, but it's going to be Blackwood."

She shook her head. "You're crazy, you know that?"

"I love you," I said it again. "I just wanted to show you that I could take care of you, that I wanted to, not because I really like having sex with you or seeing you naked."

She swatted me on the chest.

"Ouch!" I laughed. "But because you're my forever. Also, is there any better revenge than owning your ex's company?"

"How did you swing that one?"

"Investments. I always loved numbers, it was how my dad and I bonded, and then I started doing YouTube videos about money for kids, and those took off. Each time I made more, I reinvested."

"Huh?"

"I made a shit ton of money putting my brain to good use." I held up my right hand. "Swear I even had nerd fans, it was awesome."

She gaped. "You can't be serious."

"Oh, I am." I winked. "Made millions. Dad helped me invest it, and then he taught me how to trade, and I made a bit more, and well, working for Wingmen just made it better. So, if you're worried, I spent my entire life savings on revenge—don't be."

"YouTube," she repeated. "Wait, are the videos still up?"

My smile dropped. "Don't you dare—"

"Oh, I dare." She licked her lips and stood up on her tiptoes. "I'll make it worth your while."

I groaned. "One video, and if you say one thing about my missing front teeth, I'm not going to lick your—"

She clapped a hand over my mouth. "Your father is only a few feet away."

"Trust me, he's an animal. He'll understand." I shrugged, "I lived a traumatic childhood, but at least I knew my parents loved each other."

She made a face.

"Exactly." I twirled her around. "So, what do you think, professor? Should we set a date?"

"Huh?"

"Christmas wedding."

"You really are serious."

"Yup." I dipped her and pressed a soft kiss to her mouth. "I'll wear you down, don't worry..."

"You already have." She kissed me back so hard I nearly dropped her, and then I was grabbing her hand and tugging her toward the door.

"Please tell me you drove," I begged.

"No, I rode with—"

"Dad." I nodded in his direction. "Uncle Freddie's gonna take you home."

"I am?" Freddie blinked in surprise.

"He is?" Dad echoed.

"Thanks guys!" I tugged Kora toward the exit and gave the valet the ticket.

The Rolls was already parked out front for people to see, so he tossed me the keys, while I pulled out a twenty and dropped it on his stand. I glanced at Kora. "Let's go!"

Kora stared at the car, then at me. "Please tell me that's not yours."

"Dad's." I laughed. "Do I look eighty?"

She rolled her eyes and laughed. "Where are we going?"

"Your apartment. For all the sex."

"Ohhhh, he thinks he's getting sex," she mumbled with a smile.

"He knows he's getting sex. He just white knighted the shit out of Saturday." I opened her door and then pressed a hot kiss to her lips. "Any objections?"

"Hell no." She moaned into my mouth. "Drive fast."

"Planning on it."

We made it to her apartment in record time.

She jammed her key into the lock while I unzipped the back of her black dress, damn this woman and black, it was strapless and made me think of mourning.

She kicked off her heels, one landed on the couch the other on the floor and spun around to face me in nothing but a nude strapless bra and matching panties. "Leo, wait."

I already had half my tux off and was unbuttoning my

dress pants. "What? Why are we waiting?"

She dropped to her knees in front of me, grabbed my pants, and pulled them completely down.

A very excited part of me greeted her with an extremely firm hello.

She sighed, her eyes flickering up at me before I felt her mouth take me in, I was swallowed by her heat. My hands fell to her hair. "Oh, that's... words, I have no words, keep going, God keep going. I'm already so close... you make me so hot, Kora—damn, you're gonna suck me dry."

She pulled away and winked. "Kinda the point."

"I love you," I said with a groan.

And when I climaxed, she pulled back, licked her lips, and said, "I love you too."

My smile took up half my face as I pulled her to her feet and cupped her cheeks with both of my hands. "A-plus, professor Robinson, A-plus."

And then I gripped her by the ass, threw her over my shoulder, and walked into the bedroom. "Guess it's my turn to take the quiz."

I tugged her panties so hard they tore, and then my mouth got reacquainted with another favorite.

Her taste.

"Leo!" I loved the way she screamed my name.

Poor neighbors.

One day, we would move.

One day, I would buy her a house.

One day, I would fill that house with kids.

And it had all started when I fell for my teacher.

And refused to let her go.

Epilogue

"Love's a lot like falling headfirst into a never-ending black pit,
you do nothing but continue to fall,
but at least you have someone kissing you on the way down."
— Leo Blackwood

Leo

"The three musketeers are down to two." Finn glanced over at Kora and me. We were at my new penthouse, moving in a couch that I may or may not have thought through on purchasing.

It was a huge sectional that was heavy as hell.

I'd promised Slater and Finn pizza and alcohol, so they had said yes.

Our bulldog Rocky came barreling down the hall at about the same time Slater was attempting to move the final part of the couch.

"Rocky!" Slater added a few choice curse words. "Move your fat, cute ass, or you're gonna know what flat as a pancake means!"

"Rocky," I scolded. "Come here."

He didn't listen to me. Instead, he ran toward Kora, who was already sitting on part of the couch sipping wine.

"Traitor," I called after him.

Finn sighed. "Does everyone ignore me?"

"Look." I continued to watch Slater struggle. "Lex and Ian said you guys just needed to finish off the year and they'd train the new recruits at corporate. It frees up both your schedules a ton, and you only have a few months left of the semester. See? Fixed."

"Right, but there's two of us," Finn pointed out. "Which means we have more work."

"It's not that bad," Slater finally put down the sectional and then sat on it. "Plus, if it gets too hard, we can steal one of the early recruits and just assign all the easy ones."

"Ah, true." Finn yawned. "Also remember that one time Leo got friend-zoned?"

Kora shot him a look. "Who?"

"Easy green-eyed monster." Finn laughed. "I was talking about you."

"She didn't friend zone me," I argued.

"I did." She grinned.

"She did." Both Slater and Finn agreed with her.

I flipped off the room and then went to sit next to my girlfriend, soon to be fiancé. I told her I would wait a few months.

I had officially lasted one.

And I bought a ring.

Hey, when you know, you know.

It was currently burning a hole in my pocket.

So, I grabbed it and quickly dropped it into her wine glass when she wasn't looking.

The plopping sound gave it away.

"Did you just put something in my drink?" Kora glared.

"Roofied!" Slater pointed.

Finn grinned at us like he was watching a rom-com.

"Oh, look…" I pointed at her glass.

She lifted it to her face and then gasped.

I may have gone for an oval cut three karat diamond with a thin white gold band.

"Leo!" She nearly spilled her wine, and then she dipped her fingers inside the glass and pulled out the ring. "Is this what I think—"

I dropped to my knees and grabbed her free hand. "Marry me? Make me the happiest—mphhff."

Her arms wrapped around my neck so tight I had trouble breathing. "I love you so much. I love you." Her mouth found mine amidst the loud throat clearing behind us. And then we were full-on making out while the guys watched.

Hey, they could handle it.

Nothing they hadn't seen before.

We finally broke apart; her eyes were filled with happy tears. "I can't wait to marry you, I kept getting mad at myself for telling you I needed to take things slow. I don't want to wait months. I want this now."

"Me too," I said softly. "Now put on your giant ring so we can bust out the champagne."

Hands shaking, she put it on her finger. It fit perfect, although it did look a bit large on her small hand.

Good, I hope that every time that bastard Chad-dick saw her on the news or at city events he died with jealousy.

Because that was the other thing.

Now that I was out of college, I was going to a lot more charity galas with my family. I finally felt at peace.

It would be inevitable that we would see her ex.

And when we did, I fully planned on kissing the crap out of her and lifting that giant hand so the ring glittered just enough from the light—that he went blind.

See? Perfect plan.

The sound of champagne opening jolted me from my thoughts. And I smiled as my best friends celebrated with us.

The doorbell rang.

I had invited her family over along with mine, and everyone had arrived right on time, even Ian and Lex, the owners of Wingmen were going to stop by.

After all, without their app, this might not have happened.

"Dad!" Kora rushed over to her parents then to mine, and I watched with the biggest grin on my face.

Mine. She was mine.

Finally.

If you need to talk to someone, here are some resources that are available all day, every day.
Please know you are not alone.

The National Domestic Violence Hotline
We answer the call to support and shift power back to people affected by relationship abuse.
Telephone: 1-800-9-SAFE (7233)
Online chat: thehotline.org

loveisrespect
loveisrespect's purpose is to engage, educate and empower young people to prevent and end abusive relationships.
Telephone: 1-866-331-9474
Online chat: loveisrespect.org
Text: LOVEIS to 22522

Want More Pleasure Ponies?

Don't miss the Bro Code novels.
Each featuring a different member of
the Pleasure Ponies!

Co-Ed

Four guys.
Constant moaning.
And a revolving door across the college suite I somehow ended up in because my first name is Shawn.

They don't discriminate. Girls. Guys. Grandmas. Plants (okay maybe not plants) all walks of life stroll in stressed to the brim, and leave so satisfied I'm wondering what sort of talents lie behind that door.

My roommate calls them the Pleasure Ponies.
But the rest of the college campus?

They just call them the new face of Wingmen Inc. A paid for relationship service that makes big promises.

Breakup? They'll glue you back together again.
Depressed? They have the magic pill.
Lonely? Just spend a few minutes while they rub you down and you'll forget all about it.
And broken hearts? Well, that's their specialty. They'll fix you.
For a price...

I swore I wouldn't get involved.
But apparently, they like a challenge, and a girl who doesn't put up with their BS is basically like waving a red flag in front of a bull.

They. All. Charged.
But one holds my attention above the rest.

Knox Tate looks like a Viking — and getting pillaged is starting to look more appealing by the day. Though he's hiding something — all of them are. And the closer I get. The more I realize that some things are left better in the past.

Welcome to the new face of Wingmen Inc — You're welcome.

Seducing Mrs. Robinson

We've all been there, some more than others, you know what I'm talking about, where you have the hots for the new business teacher.

I was one hundred percent that guy. I shamelessly flirted with her my senior year, only earning her irritation more and more. On graduation, I stood up to her husband after he got violent, and I'll never forget the look in her eyes when she told me it wasn't my place.

Fast forward to my senior year of college and what do you know, the new adjunct professor is the one and only Mrs. Robinson, she's eight years older than me and smoking hot. Did I mention divorced?

She looks at me like I'm trouble, and I'm only happy to deliver on that promise. I'm going to show her how a real man treats a woman and use every weapon in my Pleasure Pony arsenal to do it.

Go big or go home.

Avoiding Temptation

I hit on her first.

Realized she was my best friend Finn's little sister second.

And got a bloody nose third — compliments of Finn after he watched me nearly score with the new underclassman.

After all I did have a reputation on campus, word on the street was that a girl could orgasm within one minute just watching me eat Lucky Charms.
You can't make this stuff up — even though it was at least four minutes and included outside circumstances. Ahem, I digress.

Point is, not only did I earn the attention of the worst sort of girl for me — my best friend's only sibling — but now she's out to seduce me.

Me! One of the most famous Pleasure Ponies of them all!

I can't shower — she follows me to the bathroom. Literally. I can't sleep — Lucky me, she lives in the same dorm.

And I can't focus on anything except for her taunting eyes every single time something goes her way.
I want her, but I don't want her to know I want her, and I definitely don't want to die before graduation, which is

looking more and more likely considering we can't keep our hands off each other.

Something's gotta give, and I have an inkling I should probably start writing my eulogy now because that something is probably going to be me.

The Setup

The first day she was sitting by herself — I felt sorry for her. After all, it couldn't be easy wrangling all the testosterone at Wingmen Inc as one of the only female office managers.

The second day she literally counted her carrots during break — she had seven by the way, right along with seven sips of her drink in between taking seven tiny little bites of the first carrot.

Now I'm not one to brag, or maybe I am, but math and science fascinate me, so do problems. And this woman screamed puzzle from the way she ducked her head every time anyone looked at her, to the way she counted food and tapped the table when she didn't think anyone was watching.

I'd like to think I took pity on her that day when, in fact, she was the one that took pity on me and asked if I needed a friend. She assumed I had a learning disability since I'd been staring so damn hard.

Things would have ended there, except, my bosses need someone to test the new Wingmen App and since I was the only single guy on the floor — I was nominated, right along with the only single woman, the same one who thinks I need to use my fingers to count.

Apparently rumors of my sexcapades throughout college reached even her ears, because she wants nothing to do with me, which makes beta testing a bitch. I have thirty days to win her over and prove myself to my bosses.

One thing's for certain, I'm going to have to buy a hell of a lot of carrots.

Want More Wingmen Inc?

Can't get enough of the WINGMEN?
See where it all started!

The Matchmaker's Playbook

Wingman rule number one: don't fall for a client.

After a career-ending accident, former NFL recruit Ian Hunter is back on campus—and he's ready to get his new game on. As one of the masterminds behind Wingmen, Inc., a successful and secretive word-of-mouth dating service, he's putting his extensive skills with women to work for the lovelorn. But when Blake Olson requests the services of Wingmen, Inc., Ian may have landed his most hopeless client yet.

From her frumpy athletic gear to her unfortunate choice of footwear, Blake is going to need a miracle if she wants to land her crush. At least with a professional matchmaker by her side she has a fighting chance. Ian knows that his advice and a makeover can turn Blake into another successful match. But as Blake begins the transformation from hot mess to smokin' hot, Ian realizes he's in danger of breaking his cardinal rule…

The Matchmaker's Replacement

Wingman rule number two: never reveal how much you want them.

Lex hates Gabi. Gabi hates Lex. But, hey, at least the hate is mutual, right? All Lex has to do is survive the next few weeks training Gabi in all the ways of Wingmen Inc. and then he can be done with her. But now that they have to work together, the sexual tension and fighting is off the charts. He isn't sure if he wants to strangle her or throw her against the nearest sturdy table and have his way with her.

But Gabi has a secret, something she's keeping from not just her best friend but her nemesis too. Lines are blurred as Lex becomes less the villain she's always painted him to be… and starts turning into something more. Gabi has always hated the way she's been just a little bit attracted to him— no computer-science major should have that nice of a body or look that good in glasses—but "Lex Luthor" is an evil womanizer. He's dangerous. Gabi should stay far, far away.

Then again, she's always wanted a little danger.

Acknowledgments

I'm always so thankful to God that I'm able to do what I love.

To my incredible readers I'm sorry I made you wait a whole year but now you have all three stories! Keep reading for the link to Slater's story.

As always thank you to my awesome team, and if you liked the books feel free to review, if you hated them, we still love you!

Come hang out with us at Rachels New Rockin Readers on facebook and as always follow me on insta @RachVD.

Be looking for my next release Fashion Jungle, coming soon with my writing partner Kathy Ireland!

About The Author

Rachel Van Dyken is the #1 New York Times Bestselling, Wall Street Journal, and USA Today bestselling author of over 80 books ranging from contemporary romance to paranormal. With over four million copies sold, she's been featured in Forbes, US Weekly, and USA Today. Her books have been translated in more than 15 countries. She was one of the first romance authors to have a Kindle in Motion book through Amazon publishing and continues to strive to be on the cutting edge of the reader experience. She keeps her home in the Pacific Northwest with her husband, adorable son, naked cat, and two dogs. For more information about her books and upcoming events, visit www.RachelVanDykenauthor.com.

Also By Rachel Van Dyken

Kathy Ireland & Rachel Van Dyken
Fashion Jungle

Eagle Elite
Elite
Elect
Entice
Elicit
Bang Bang
Enforce
Ember
Elude
Empire
Enrage
Eulogy
Envy

Elite Bratva Brotherhood
RIP
Debase

The Bet Series
The Bet
The Wager
The Dare

Seaside Series
Tear
Pull
Shatter
Forever
Fall
Strung
Eternal

Seaside Pictures
Capture
Keep
Steal
All Stars Fall
Abandon

Ruin Series
Ruin
Toxic
Fearless
Shame

Covet
Stealing Her
Finding Him

The Consequence Series

The Consequence of Loving Colton
The Consequence of Revenge
The Consequence of Seduction
The Consequence of Rejection

The Dark Ones Series

The Dark Ones
Untouchable Darkness
Dark Surrender
Darkest Temptation

Wingmen Inc.

The Matchmaker's Playbook
The Matchmaker's Replacement

Bro Code

Co-Ed
Seducing Mrs. Robinson
Avoiding Temptation
The Setup

The Bachelors of Arizona

The Bachelor Auction
The Playboy Bachelor
The Bachelor Contract

Curious Liaisons

Cheater
Cheater's Regret

Players Game
Fraternize
Infraction
M.V.P.

Red Card
Risky Play
Kickin' It

Liars, Inc
Dirty Exes
Dangerous Exes

Cruel Summer
Summer Heat
Summer Seduction
Summer Nights

Waltzing With The Wallflower
Waltzing with the Wallflower
Beguiling Bridget
Taming Wilde

London Fairy Tales
Upon a Midnight Dream
Whispered Music
The Wolf's Pursuit
When Ash Falls

Renwick House

The Ugly Duckling Debutante
The Seduction of Sebastian St. James
The Redemption of Lord Rawlings
An Unlikely Alliance
The Devil Duke Takes a Bride

Other Titles

The Parting Gift
Compromising Kessen
Savage Winter
Divine Uprising
Every Girl Does It
A Crown for Christmas

RACHEL VAN DYKEN BOOKS

Made in the USA
Monee, IL
02 July 2020